THE GHOST GROOM

JENNIFER YOUNGBLOOD

ARBOR
HOUSE

This was such a fun book to write. I loved all the twists and turns. And, I enjoyed adding in the section about paramotoring.

It's interesting how things come about. I had no idea when I let my son borrow my car and he took it to a college campus where another student backed over the passenger side that it would lead me to paramotoring. Let me explain ... My son was horrified about the accident, but it wasn't his fault. The Honda was parked when it happened. The girl who ran over our car was kind enough to leave her name and number so we could contact her insurance company.

We took the Honda to a highly recommended bodyshop guy named Russ Bateman. Russ and I struck up a conversation, through which I learned that he's a certified paramotoring instructor. What is paramotoring, you may ask? In layman's terms it's paragliding with a motor.

Russ and his son Dallin were kind enough to let me interview them at their home. Hearing Russ and Dallin talk about paramotoring made me want to try it. I haven't yet due to the frigid weather this time of year. But I'm working up the courage to give it a go this spring.

I love researching unusual topics for my books and felt privileged to get the inside track on this not-so-well-known sport. According to Russ, in France during the summer, there are on average forty-seven thousand registered pilots as opposed to roughly eight thousand in the US.

Thanks, Russ and Dallin, for taking the time to educate me about paramotoring so I could share it with my readers! (And sound halfway intelligent about it.) LOL

MY GIFT TO YOU ...

Get Beastly Charm: A Contemporary retelling of beauty & the beast as a welcome gift when you sign up for my newsletter. You'll get information on my new releases, book recommendations, discounts, and other freebies.

Get the book at:

http://bit.ly/freebookjenniferyoungblood

1

Bass from the music thudded in Ariana's chest like a second heartbeat as she threaded her way through the crowded club, searching for the man she was supposed to meet. They'd agreed on 7:30 and twenty minutes had passed since then, not a great start for a first date. She glanced back toward the bar where she'd been sitting. A guy with long, stringy hair was talking to a woman beside him. The guy was into the conversation, but the woman looked bored. A few seats over, an older man with his head down was downing shots like water. No sign of Justin.

Ariana wasn't crazy about the club scene, but she loved to dance. Supposedly her date, Justin, did too, which is why they'd planned to meet here. Plus, she had a fun surprise planned for Justin, something that would be right up his alley. If only he'd get here, they might just have a decent date. Although Ariana was on a streak of rotten luck where men were concerned. It all started when she and Paul broke up, and went downhill from there.

At first, she'd hoped maybe Paul was "the one," but after a few months of dating their relationship stagnated. Their breakup was a mutual thing, but a part of her missed Paul. Well, maybe not him, necessarily. But she missed having someone in her life. An insurance attorney, Paul was a nice guy, but married to his work ... and kind of dull. She felt guilty even thinking that, but it was true. After the breakup, Ariana went on a handful of dates each month, but hadn't met anyone she gelled with. Most of the dates had been so awkward, Ariana was starting to wonder if she'd ever find anyone.

She'd been cautiously optimistic about the Heart to Heart App everyone at her gym raved about. A local company developed it as a way for singles in Dallas and Ft. Worth to connect. The app premise focused on the inner qualities of the person rather than the outward appearance, hence no photos. Couples were matched through an algorithm combined with a professional staff assessing the individuals' compatibility. While that sounded good in theory, Ariana also knew physical attraction played a large part in a relationship. So, after she and Justin "matched" and began texting back and forth, they shared photos.

Ariana was pleasantly surprised to find Justin a handsome man, not movie-star handsome, but good looking enough. She'd never been into the pretty-boy types and wanted to find someone down-to-earth who enjoyed similar activities. From what she could tell, Justin fit the bill. He enjoyed dancing, rock climbing, kickboxing, but also, photography and museums. In fact, Justin's interests were so similar to hers that she wondered if he might be too good to be true. Well, there was his profession, which she wasn't too keen on. But she was willing to overlook that due to his other qualities. Supposedly, he was a karaoke ninja. She'd find out about that one shortly, if the dude ever got here. Punctuality certainly wasn't one of his strengths.

Irritation prickled through her. *Strike One*. She reached in her purse to grab her phone. She'd sent him a text earlier, but he hadn't responded. Maybe now ... Yep. There was a text.

Running late. Got held up at the office. Be there by 8:15.

Really? 8:15? That meant she still had about thirty minutes to kill. *Great. Now what?*

Twenty-five minutes later, Ariana was sitting at a table, slurping the remains of a Dr. Pepper through a straw when she saw the guy dancing. About six feet tall with a fit, muscular build, he had curly, dark-blonde hair with sun-bleached ends. A jolt shot through Ariana with enough juice to jumpstart a semi-truck as she watched him tear up the dance floor, his curls bouncing with every movement. Had he not been dancing with another girl, she might've obeyed the impulse to spring out of her chair and join him.

It wasn't that the guy had the best moves on the floor, but he was so fluid and charismatic, like he was living totally in the moment. Her gaze took in his even features. He was good-looking with a strong chin, maybe a little too good-looking for her taste. Unlike most pretty boys, so preoccupied with how they appeared to others they could hardly make a move, this guy seemed oblivious to what people thought of him. He was simply living in the moment, pouring a week's worth of passion into that one dance. The girl he was with was losing steam, but not him. He looked like he could dance at that pace all night. Ariana jerked, tightening her hold on her drink, when his eyes locked with hers. She was shocked at the energy that buzzed through her. Her throat went dry as she swallowed.

He smiled.

She smiled back, going warm all over.

His dance partner followed his trail of vision, and then frowned, glaring at Ariana.

Ariana glanced down, breaking the connection. Everything in her wanted to keep staring at him, but that would be in poor taste. He was with another girl. She stirred her straw through the melted ice cubes. For all she knew the guy could be engaged to the other girl ... or married. And she was making moon eyes at him. She tugged at her dress. Where in the heck was Justin? She allowed herself one more look at the guy. Thankfully, he had his back facing her. Sheesh. He had broad shoulders that tapered in to his waist. She knew plenty of guys who'd kill for a body like that. She tore her eyes away from him, not wanting his date to catch her watching him.

Someone touched her shoulder. "Hello."

She looked up. "Hey, Justin," she said as she got to her feet and gave him a quick hug. He pulled out a chair and sat down across from her.

"I'm sorry I'm late," he began. "The summer training camp ran longer than I expected. And traffic was a beast."

Justin was a high school football coach. She'd had terrible luck dating football players.

She'd almost cancelled their date when she realized what Justin did professionally, but they seemed so well suited in other areas that she thought it might be okay. She forced a smile. "It's fine." She held up her glass, chuckling. "I had the Dr. to keep me company."

He tilted his head in confusion. "I'm sorry."

"Dr. Pepper," she explained.

"Oh." He gave her a courtesy smile.

She lifted the glass to her lips and swallowed down her disappointment with the remaining liquid. Justin was a good thirty pounds heavier than he'd appeared in his pictures with graying temples—which in and of itself was okay. But it was concerning that he'd portrayed himself so differently. She glanced toward the dance floor. The guy was no longer there. She sighed resolutely. It was probably a good thing. Otherwise, she would've had a hard time focusing on Justin. A part of her wondered if she should use Justin's tardiness as an excuse to end the date and go home. Then again, she was here, so she might as well make the best of the evening. Better to be here than sitting at home, watching TV.

Justin was eyeing her with open admiration that bordered on leering.

She cocked an eyebrow, a smile straining over her lips as she touched her hair. "What?"

"You're flipping gorgeous."

"Thanks." The brazen way he was staring at her was making her uncomfortable.

He placed a hand over hers as he leaned forward, innuendo in his voice. "I'm so glad we matched."

She removed her hand. *Down, boy.* "Should I order you something to drink?"

"That would be great."

Before she could make a move, he lifted his hand, signaling to the server. "Hey, over here," he boomed, snapping his fingers, like he was summoning a servant.

Ariana bristled in surprise.

The server, a young girl in her early twenties, stepped up to the table.

Justin flashed a broad smile. "Two beers."

"Oh, I don't drink alcohol," Ariana said.

"Those were both for me." Justin winked at the server, his eyes lingering on her slim hips. "Thanks, sugar. Hurry back." He drummed his fingers on the table to the beat of the music.

Okay, this guy was starting to get on her nerves. Talk about an overgrown frat boy. Ariana sat back in her seat and folded her arms over her chest, eyeing him. "I'd love to see your photographs. Do you use a Sony or Canon?"

His eyes widened. "A cannon for what?"

"What kind of camera do you shoot with?" Justin didn't have a clue about photography. She wondered what else he'd lied about. "On your profile, you mentioned that you take pictures."

"Oh, yeah. That." He offered a sheepish grin. "I mostly take pictures with my iPhone."

She eyed him. "And you're into kickboxing and rock climbing? At least, according to your profile."

"Sure, I do both of those things." He leaned in. "I'll kickbox with you any day, baby."

A brittle laugh rumbled in her throat. "First of all, I'm not your baby."

He held up a hand. "Settle down. I meant no offense. It was a compliment."

She just looked at him, her eyebrow raised.

"So you own a gym? That's really cool."

She relaxed a fraction. "Yeah, it is cool."

His eyes moved over her. "No wonder you look so great. I mean, normally I like girls with longer hair. But that pixie thing you have going is kind of sexy."

Was this guy for real? She was tempted to say that she normally liked guys who had an IQ greater than a hundred, but didn't want to be rude. She touched her hair, which was longer on top and tapered around her ears. She practically lived in workout clothes, and it was easier to keep her hair short so that it was out of the way. Plus, short hair fit her personality.

The server returned with the beers. Justin downed the first one in two minutes flat.

"I'm surprised to see you drinking. When we texted, you said you didn't drink because it interfered with your fitness regimen." Even as she spoke the words, it went through her mind that the only fitness regimen Justin had been doing was probably flipping TV channels and shoveling potato chips into his mouth.

Justin was lifting the second mug to his lips and froze, putting it back down on the table. He grunted. "You must be mistaken. I never said that."

"Yes, you did." *Strike two.* "You know, Justin. I don't think this is a good idea. Maybe we should just call it a night." She moved to stand, but he caught her arm.

"Let's just dance a little, okay? I mean, we're here. Right?"

"Let go of my arm."

He held up his hand. "I didn't mean anything by it. I really wish you'd stay though." He smiled. "Dancing is something I do know how to do." He made a dancing motion with his hands. "When you see these moves, you'll be swimming in adoration."

She couldn't help but chuckle in mild amusement. The guy had a Texas-sized ego. Yeah, he'd probably been something to look at ... a decade ago. He wasn't bad looking now, even with the extra weight. It was his jock attitude that was getting under her skin. "All right." She sat back down. The only reason she agreed to stay was to see the look on Justin's face when he realized that she'd signed them up to do a karaoke duet. He'd lied about everything else, so she was pretty sure all that talk about being a karaoke ninja was a load of crap, but it might be entertaining to see him fumble through it.

Justin took a long drink from the second mug, then put it down on the table with a loud plop. He jumped up. "Let's go. I promise you. You're going to be amazed."

She rolled her eyes. "I seriously doubt that," she muttered under her breath.

RENNEN SCOPED THE ROOM, looking for the vivacious brunette he'd seen earlier. She was no longer sitting at the table. He'd planned on going over to talk to her after the song ended, but then she was with another guy. He'd come here tonight with a couple of buddies, and assumed they'd hang out and talk, maybe share a few laughs. But his buddies had latched onto girls almost from the moment they got here, leaving him to fend for himself. Rennen loved dancing, so that was one consolation.

The brunette appeared about ten feet from where he was standing. She was dancing with the same guy who'd sat down at the table with her. Were they together? She was stunningly beautiful with lively dark eyes, a sculpted nose, and generous mouth. Her cheeks were rosy with heightened color from the physical exertion. She was petite and curvy in all the right places, moving effortlessly in her stilettos. Long silver earrings dangled beneath her stylishly-cut hair. A spark of attraction had shot through him earlier when their eyes connected and she smiled at him. She was dancing circles around her partner, making him look like a big oaf in comparison. Rennen wondered if he should try and cut in. The worst that could happen was that the girl would tell him they were together. No, the more Rennen watched them, the more he got the feeling they weren't a couple. In fact, the guy kept attempting to move in and put his hands on her, but she evaded him. An unreasonable surge of jealousy sparked through Rennen when the guy put a hand on her waist. This time, she took his hand and removed it, scowling.

Rennen's jaw tightened as he stepped closer. He'd watch the situation for a couple of seconds longer to make sure he was reading things correctly. And then he'd intervene and save her from being mauled.

THIS WAS GETTING RIDICULOUS. Justin was more handsy than an octopus. "Stop touching me," she warned.

He laughed. "Come on, babe. Don't be so stiff. You know you like it."

"No, I don't like it," she countered. "No one likes being pawed." Revulsion churned in her gut as his eyes went to her chest. An incredulous laugh bubbled in her throat. Was he really ogling her chest, right here in front of her? What a jerk! As soon as she got home, she was going to contact Heart to Heart and put in a complaint. They really should be more diligent in making sure people were truthful in their profiles. Justin was nothing like he'd pretended to be, and it was obvious he was only after one thing ... and it wasn't a long-term relationship. She tensed, clenching her fists. "Hey, buddy. My face is up here."

He snorted out a chortle. "Yeah, but you've got something else going on down there. For a little girl, you've got a nice rack."

She froze amidst the dancing couples surrounding them. "What did you just say to me?"

He laughed. "You heard me. Lighten up." He grabbed her waist with an iron grip. "I thought Latin girls were supposed to be loose."

Her hand balled into a fist, and she thought about how it would feel to knock him across the floor. "I'm going to give you a half a second to let go of me."

He grunted in amusement. "Make me."

Heat splintered up her neck, making her feel like her head would split in two. Then cool precision took over as she calculated Justin's height and weight. *The bigger they are ... the harder they fall.* From the corner of her eye, she saw the blonde guy from earlier approach. "Is everything okay here?" he asked, his body taut, like he was ready to pounce.

"Buzz off," Justin grumbled. Letting loose a string of curse words.

"Strike three," Ariana muttered. She shot her arm straight up in a swift motion where it connected with Justin's neck, right under his jaw line. Then she brought her arm back down, using her weight to knock him off his feet where he landed on his back with a heavy thud. Murmurs rippled through the couples surrounding them as they backed away. Justin gurgled, clutching his neck, a dazed look in his eyes.

Ariana's hands flew to her hips. "Just because I'm Latin does not make me easy!"

Claps broke out around her. "That's right," a few of the women agreed. "Dirt bag," one woman muttered, shooting Justin a death glare.

As Justin stumbled to his feet, Ariana planted herself in a battle stance, ready to do more damage if necessary. Her adrenaline was going, and she'd make short work of him, putting her training to good use. But luckily for Justin, he ducked his head and scuttled away.

"That has got to be the most awesome thing I've ever seen."

She turned to the blonde guy who was looking at her in astonishment, admiration shining in his eyes. "Thanks. I appreciate you trying to help."

He shoved his hands in his pockets, rocking forward on the balls of his feet. "Yeah, I was trying to rescue you from that creep ... not that you needed my help."

Ariana's blood was pumping so ferociously that she felt dizzy.

He gave her a concerned look. "Are you okay?"

A wan smile tipped her lips as she ran a hand through her hair. "Yeah, I guess that date didn't go as planned."

He chuckled. "Life rarely does." He held her gaze, and she felt the same buzz she'd experienced earlier. Everything around them slowed, and it was just the two of them. His voice was deeper than she imagined, with a husky edge. Her eyes traced the definition of the muscles underneath his form-fitting t-shirt. Heat fanned her face when she saw the flicker of amusement that turned his hazel-green eyes a honey-gold. He'd caught her checking him out. She jerked her eyes to his face, making a mental note to keep her focus there. He had a fine layer of scruff, emphasizing the lean line of his jaw. She swallowed, feeling she was staring at the real-life version of Thor and Captain America, all rolled into one. *Captain Thor*. Or Goldie Locks because of his thick tangles of beautiful curls.

People around them resumed dancing, but the two of them just stood there. Ariana knew she should start dancing ... or do something to break the tension, but she couldn't get her body to cooperate.

He cleared his throat, a grin washing over his face. "Um, maybe we should get off the dance floor."

"Oh, yeah." She propelled her feet into action. Her mind whirled, going through all that had just happened. She could hardly believe he'd been the one to offer help. When they got to the side, he motioned to an empty table.

"Would you like to sit down?"

Her voice sounded unnaturally high and screechy in her ears. "Sure."

He pulled out a chair for her and helped her get seated. Wow. Captain Thor was a gentleman to the nth degree. A startling contrast to Justin.

As they sat there, staring across the table at each other, Ariana scrambled for something halfway intelligent to say. "Thanks again. You're a great dancer," she blurted. *Sheesh*. She was making an idiot out of herself. Normally she was calm and cool around men, always knowing the right thing to say. But it seemed her mouth had disconnected from her brain.

His lips curved into a radiant smile, causing the edges of his eyes to crease. "Thanks. You're pretty good yourself."

The compliment caught her off guard, sending warm ripples cascading through her. He'd been watching her too. It was good to know the attraction went both ways.

He leaned forward. "Was that guy your boyfriend?"

She wrinkled her nose. "Heck no!" She laughed. "We'd never met in person before tonight. We were matched on a dating app."

His eyebrows shot up in surprise. "Really?"

She felt foolish and a little desperate for resorting to a dating app. Her explanation gushed out. "It's an app where people in the Dallas/Ft. Worth area can connect. You know, people with similar interests." She shrugged. "It seemed like a good idea ... in theory." She scowled, darkness gathering inside her. "Of course, I should've known better than to go out with a football coach. Note to self ... don't date anymore coaches or football players. Their egos are the size of a whale, their brains the size of a pea, from one too many hits on the field."

He laughed. "That's a bit of a blanket statement."

Her face fell. "Don't tell me, you're a football player." Of course he was. That would be just her luck.

An easy grin stole over his lips. "Well, if I were, I certainly wouldn't admit it now."

She pursed her lips together, assessing him. He didn't seem bothered by her scrutiny. He just sat there, patiently enduring it. "No, you're not a football player," she finally said. "I don't know what you are, but you're far too intelligent to play football."

He cocked his head. "So, all football players are stupid? Is that what you're saying?"

"Nope. Not all of them. Just about ninety percent."

"So only ten percent are intelligent." He grinned. "See, I can do math."

The teasing tone of his voice caused her to smile. "That's good to know."

He tsked his tongue. "What turned you against football players?"

"Aside from Justin?" She lifted an eyebrow, waiting for him to respond.

"Yep, aside from him. I mean, he was a douche bag, but the bite in your voice tells me there's more."

When her brother Ace first started playing pro ball, Ariana went out with a few players on the team. After about the sixth disaster, she swore off football players altogether. "Experience," she finally said.

Interest lit his eyes. "Care to elaborate?"

"Not really," she said loudly, then felt like she was yelling when the music suddenly stopped.

They turned their attention to the guy on stage holding the microphone. "Folks, we've got a fun evening lined up, it's karaoke night!" He pumped a fist in the air as the crowd cheered.

Ariana's heart dropped. *Oh, no!*

The emcee looked down at the sheet of paper in his hand. "To start, we have a duet by Ariana and Justin."

Captain Thor looked at her. "Is everything okay?"

"Not really." She groaned. "I'm Ariana."

His eyes widened, then he burst out laughing, a deep throaty laugh that rumbled in his chest. "And the jerk you laid out is Justin."

She smiled thinly. "Yep." She let out a heavy sigh. "This night just keeps getting better and better."

"Ladies and gentlemen," the emcee said, "give it up for Ariana and Justin. They'll be doing an oldie but goodie, *Eye of the Tiger*."

A roar of clapping circled through the room.

Ariana's heart hammered against her ribcage. She glanced at the exit door. It wasn't too late to make a run for it. No one knew she was Ariana. Well, except for Captain Thor. She really didn't care what the people in the club thought about her. But for some strange reason, she cared what he thought. Before her mind processed what she was doing, she was on her feet and making her way to the stage. She'd done karaoke enough times to know she could hold her own. Even so, her hand shook slightly when she took the microphone. "I'm Ariana," she said, pointing to her chest. She plastered on a cheerful smile. "Unfortunately, Justin had to leave, so it'll just be me tonight."

Boos rumbled through the audience.

The emcee held up a hand. "Hey, y'all. Show the lady some respect. It takes a lot of guts to come up here and perform in front of a bunch of yahoos. Give it up for Ariana!" He brought his hands together in vigorous claps that started the audience clapping.

Ariana was glad the stage lights were shining in her eyes, preventing her from seeing Captain Thor's expression. He probably thought she was loco. The lyrics popped up on the screen. She gripped the microphone, trying to get in the proper frame of mind to perform.

"Wait a minute! What's this?" the emcee said. "It looks like Justin's here after all."

Ariana's heart lurched. *What?* She was going to lay Justin out flat, right here on stage. In the next second, a burst of sheer exhilaration ran through her when Captain Thor stepped up beside her. "Hey," she said, unable to stop a grin from spilling over her lips. "What're you doing?"

He winked. "Rescuing you."

She felt light enough to float. A giggle escaped her throat. "Do you karaoke?"

The emcee handed him a microphone as he looked at the screen. "I guess we're about to find out."

"Ariana and Justin," the emcee announced.

"The name's Rennen."

"Rennen." Ariana committed the name to memory. It fit him.

2

Rennen probably should've thought this through before hopping up on stage. When he heard the slight quiver in Ariana's voice as she explained that she'd be singing solo, instinct took over and he sprang into action. Rennen was used to jumping full force into stressful situations and making things work. He'd spent his entire life fighting for every little thing, but he didn't often go looking for ways to put himself in awkward situations. And yet, he'd felt compelled to help Ariana, a girl he didn't even know, twice in less than 30 minutes. *Interesting.*

The music started. He fumbled the beginning, mumbling through the first few lines. But he gained confidence as the song progressed. The audience clapped along with the music, helping him feel even better. By the end of the first section, Rennen was feeling pretty good about things. The charge of energy rushing through him was akin to what he felt on the field, that moment when he could see everything from the beginning to the end, knowing he had it in him to sail past the obstacles for the touchdown.

The crowd went wild when he started dancing and did a slide movement to the side. Ariana's eyes locked with his as she tilted her head back and gave him an appreciative smile that caught the light.

Heck. He'd do a thousand rounds of karaoke to earn another smile like that.

It was Ariana's turn to sing. He marveled at how she had the crowd eating out of the palm of her hand. He'd heard it said once that dynamite comes in small packages. That was indeed the case with Ariana. She was a fascinating combination of toughness and beauty, the picture of grace as she moved fluidly in her heels. He couldn't get over how effortlessly she'd taken Justin down.

When they reached the chorus, they leaned together and sang in unison. Rennen was pleasantly surprised at how well their voices blended. The music took over as he moved along with the rhythm, doing the motions that felt natural. There was something so liberating about the experience that he almost felt like a rock star, belting out the lyrics. He'd not wanted to come here tonight, but his buddies had talked him into it, accusing him of being too much of a homebody. But once he got here and started dancing, he felt like he was sixteen again. He'd forgotten how much he loved to dance. It was good to immerse himself in the moment and forget about the stress in his life. The intensity in the room escalated to a throbbing pulse, taking on a life of its own. At the end of the song, Ariana took his hand and raised it high in the air. The audience jumped to their feet, giving them a standing ovation.

A burst of pride shot through Rennen as they took a bow. The emcee jogged over to them, clapping. "That was fantastic!" he beamed. "One of the best performances I've ever seen." He turned to the audience. "Ariana and Rennen," he proclaimed.

A roar went through the room. As they exited the stage, people patted their shoulders. All Rennen could think about was how Ariana was still holding his hand, the warmth of her touch seeping through his skin. He loved how tiny her hand felt in his; and yet, her grip was firm, determined. When they reached their table, she released his hand and cleared her throat like she'd just now realized she was still holding it. They sat down at the table as another couple took the stage. Rennen had worked up a sweat, and the stuffy room wasn't helping matters. Ariana seemed to be reading his mind as she fanned her face with her hands. "You wanna go outside and get cooled off?"

He grinned. "I thought you'd never ask."

It was a little cooler outside but not much. The air still held the balmy heat from earlier in the day. Texas summers were relentless as far as heat went, but Rennen was used to it, having grown up in Austin. Rennen mostly liked being outside because that meant he could be alone with Ariana to get to know her better, away from the crowd and loud music.

Ariana glanced up at him. "Where to?"

Good question. Rennen looked out over the parking lot, packed with cars. "We can go over and stand by my car."

She nodded. "Sounds good to me."

Rennen led her to his car, wondering how she'd react to his red, Nissan Z sports car. Most girls went gaga over it, but he got the feeling Ariana might think it was too showy.

"This is your car?" She cocked an eyebrow, amusement sparking in her dark eyes.

"Yep, afraid so." He forced a smile. Just as he suspected. She was not the least bit impressed. Disappointment gathered in his throat as he swallowed. "You don't like it?" He rested his back against the door, crossing his arms over his chest.

"Mind if I put my purse on it?"

"No, not at all."

"You sure? I'd hate to smudge that fancy wax job. Did you spit-shine it before you came?"

He tensed, then saw the laughter in her eyes and realized she was teasing him. He relaxed a fraction, but still didn't like that she was dissing his car.

"Sorry." She winked, giving his arm a slight shove before placing her purse on the hood. "I couldn't resist." She leaned back against the car, standing next to him. "It's a beautiful car. Just a little flashy for my taste."

He turned to her, his gaze taking in her exotic features and soulful eyes. *You're just the right amount of flashy for my taste*, he wanted to say.

Electricity thrummed through his veins as he leaned closer, his eyes tracing the outline of her delicate jaw, the stubborn set of her chin, her irresistible mouth, perfect for kissing. It wasn't like him to charge this fast into the unknown with a woman, but there was something about Ariana that made him feel reckless. Maybe it was because she was so vivacious with her conquer-the-world attitude. "What exactly is your taste?" he murmured. Her breath caught, and for a moment he feared he'd misread the situation, coming on too strong. But a tiny smile touched her lips, her eyes lighting with anticipation.

"I like tall, rugged blondes," she uttered in a throaty voice that sent his cells swirling. Her eyes caressed his. He could get lost in the depth of those mysterious eyes. "Great dancers that can hold their own on the karaoke stage." A full smile broke over her lips. "You were awesome, by the way."

He slipped his arm around her tiny waist. "All I had to do was follow your lead." They fit together so well. She was so petite, yet muscular. Her sexy, stylish bangs framed her face perfectly. A car pulled into the parking lot, the headlights reflecting off her dangly earrings, drawing attention to her slender neck and collarbone. "How do you feel about kissing on the first date?"

She laughed softly, the flats of her palms resting on his chest. "I don't think this qualifies as a first date."

"Okay, how do you feel about kissing before the first date?"

She drew her mouth together in a mock frown. "Normally, I'd say no." Mischief sparkled in her eyes. "But try me."

That's all the prompting he needed. When his lips touched hers, an explosion of pulses rocketed through him. She responded by threading her arms around his neck and pulling him closer. He ran his hands up her back and through her silky hair. Adrenaline surged through him as he deepened the kiss, their mouths moving together in a fiery dance. She met him measure for measure until he thought he'd melt from the intensity. When he pulled back, they were both breathing hard.

He grinned, his hands cupping her cheeks. "Wow, you're incredible."

A smile curved her lips. "You're not so bad yourself."

When he left his condo this evening, he couldn't have imagined the night would end like this. His heart swelled two sizes. She scooted into the curve of his shoulder as he draped his arm around her. He reached for her hand, linking her fingers through his. "I want to know everything about you."

She chuckled. "If I tell you everything in one swoop, we won't have anything else to talk about when we go out again."

He soared, loving the sound of this. "Again? I thought this didn't qualify as a first date."

"Oh, yeah. It doesn't. When we go out, I want the works—you picking me up at the door and taking me out for a nice dinner. Maybe even flowers and chocolate."

She was so adorable, ticking off her expectations. Normally, Rennen had a hard time connecting with people right off the bat. He was surprised how comfortable he felt with Ariana. And that kiss. Wow! She was really something! The parking lot was dark enough to allow them a splendid view of the glittering stars, which spanned endlessly in the velvety sky. Rennen felt light enough to fly to the stars. He could hardly believe this was happening. It was obvious Ariana had no idea who he was and that she liked him for himself, plain Rennen. This was good. Very good. Although she wouldn't be happy when she found out about his profession. Maybe he'd keep that to himself until she got to know him better. He drew his lips together thoughtfully. "Hmm ... flowers and chocolate. Maybe we should save those for dates two and three."

"Yeah, maybe," she laughed. "I'd hate to break the bank." She gave him an impish grin, cutting her eyes at his car. "After all, I'm sure this bad boy comes with a hefty payment."

"Hey, now," he drawled, "quit bagging on Red."

She gawked. "You named your car?"

"Of course."

She shook her head. "Oh, boy. This is worse than I thought. Maybe I should leave the two of you alone." She leaned forward like she was going to make a break for it, but he tightened his hold on her hand.

"Hey, now. You can't leave me here by myself."

She laughed. "I'm sure you'd survive."

The irony of her phrase hit him full force. Survival had been the name of his game for as long as he could remember. That's how he rolled. Pushing forward against all opposition, suppressing his inner-feelings. Never letting himself get too attached to anyone. But somehow, it felt different with Ariana. "What kind of car do you drive?"

"For your information, I don't drive a car. I have a truck. Four-wheel drive."

"Really? What's a sweet, little girl like you doing with a truck?"

"Who says I'm sweet?" she retorted.

He laughed, loving her spunk. "You make a good point. You laid the football coach out in two-seconds flat."

The corners of her lips turned down. "He deserved it."

Rennen tsked his tongue. "Remind me not to get on your bad side. Speaking of the coach, there's something I've been wondering."

"What?"

"Why did you go through a dating service?" He saw her expression tense and rushed to explain himself. "I mean, you're incredible."

She smiled, her features relaxing. "Thanks."

"I'm sure you have the guys lining up to date you."

There was a long pause before she spoke, and he could tell she was collecting her thoughts. She let go of his hand and moved so that he was forced to remove his arm from her shoulders. "It's hard to find good guys. There are so many creeps out there. My clients at the gym kept raving about Heart to Heart, so I thought I'd give it a try." She chuckled dryly. "It wasn't what it was cracked up to be … obviously." She grew thoughtful. "The idea behind the app is good, if people are truthful when they fill out their profiles. The idea is to match people's interests, focus more on the inner person rather than just outward appearance."

"Do you think you'll try again?" He held his breath, waiting for her answer.

She shrugged. "I dunno. Maybe. I signed a three-month contract. I guess I'll just have to see how it goes."

He nodded, trying to keep his expression neutral. It was surprising how much the idea of Ariana dating other guys bothered him. Not that he had any claim on her. They'd only just met. But that kiss had lit him on fire. It meant something to him. He could only hope Ariana felt the same way. Girls like her didn't come along every day. He'd never met anyone like Ariana—so comfortable in her own skin, so full of life. He went back to something she said. "Do you work at a gym?" That would explain why she was in such excellent shape.

A quirky smile tugged at her lips. "Yeah, sort of ..."

"Spit it out," he prompted.

"I own a gym."

Pride shone in her eyes, even though Rennen could tell she was trying to be low key about it. "Wow, that's awesome. I'll have to go there and work out sometime."

Amusement touched her eyes. "You should. I'll put you through a couple of classes. See how you measure up."

"What do you offer?"

"Kickboxing, Zumba, spin, circuit, high-intensity cardio. It runs the gamut."

"I'm assuming from the way you handled yourself earlier that you also teach self-defense classes?"

She lifted her chin. "Yep."

He shook his head, a smile sliding over his lips. "The poor coach didn't know what he was getting himself into."

She arched an eyebrow, fire sparking in her eyes. "Well, he should have the moment he referred to my breasts as a rack."

Rennen's eyes widened as he burst out laughing. "Are you serious?"

Ariana also laughed. "Yes, can you believe that?"

"What a tool," he muttered, shaking his head. "It's a good thing you took him out. Maybe he'll think twice before insulting some other poor girl."

"I doubt it," she said dryly.

Rennen couldn't remember the last time he'd been this fascinated by a woman. He wanted to know everything about Ariana. A million questions popped through his mind. He studied her. "What are your favorite foods? What do you enjoy doing when you're not working? Tell me about your family."

She laughed. "Whoa, hold your horses. I don't just want to talk about me. I wanna know about you."

His jaw tightened as he tried to figure out a way to navigate around his profession—the thing that consumed every waking hour of his life. If he told Ariana the truth, she'd be done with him.

"What's your last name?"

Had she heard of him? Probably. Briefly, he thought about giving her a fake name, but that would only make things more difficult. "Bradley." He braced for her reaction.

"Rennen Bradley." She assessed him. "It suits you."

He relaxed and then jerked back to attention at her next comment.

"Your name sounds so familiar," she mused. "Where have I heard it?"

For the past few months, Rennen's name had been plastered over every sports channel known to man. He forced a smile. "I dunno."

She scrunched her brows. "It'll come to me eventually."

If she Googled his name, she'd know who he was in an instant. But maybe she wouldn't think to do that. To her, he was just an average guy.

Quickly, he changed the subject. "What's your last name?"

"Sanchez."

His pulse picked up a notch. No, it couldn't be! Fate wouldn't be this cruel. Sanchez was a common name. There were probably hundreds, if not thousands of people with the last name Sanchez in the Metroplex alone.

She groaned. "I can tell by your expression that you're putting it together."

His throat went drier than a Texas field in July. "What do you mean?"

"Yes, I'm related to Ace Sanchez. He's my brother." She made a face. "I figured I might as well come out with it right now and save us some time."

Hot needles pelted Rennen, then he went cold. This couldn't be happening! Of all the people for him to meet, why did it have to be Ace's sister?

"Are you okay?" She gave him a funny look. "Do you know Ace?"

He forced a laugh. "I'm sure all of Texas knows your brother."

She nodded. "Now you know the real reason I like going through an app to get a date. At least that way, I'll know the guy wants to go out with me for me, not because he wants to buddy up to my brother."

"Makes sense." If only Ariana knew how much they had in common. She'd hate him when she learned who he was. He tried to keep his expression benign, even though his head was swimming. "Does your distaste for football players have something to do with your brother?"

Her brows furrowed. "Sort of." She waved a hand. "Ace is a great guy. I love him to pieces. Unfortunately, not all players are like him. Most of them are self-centered and cocky with very little upstairs." She pointed to her temple. "Anyway, enough about that. Sorry, I didn't mean to get off on a tangent." She paused, looking at him thoughtfully. "Are you a fan of football?"

"I watch an occasional game now and then," he said casually. Lightning was going to bolt through the sky and strike him dead.

A smile played on her lips. "Just do me one favor, okay?"

"Sure." His pulse pounded in his temples.

"Don't make a big deal about Ace when you meet him. Treat him like a regular guy."

He nodded.

"And whatever you do, please don't say anything about his injury or how he's no longer playing for the Titans. Ace tries to act like it's no big deal, but it's tearing him up inside."

"I certainly won't mention anything about that." Sweat beaded across the bridge of his nose. He hoped the semi-darkness would hide it.

"Enough about me. I want to hear all about you, Rennen Bradley. What do you do for a living?"

Rennen got the feeling he was standing on a ledge. A gun was pointed at him and his only two options were to get shot or jump. He let out a nervous laugh. "It's funny you'd bring up football—"

Ariana's phone rang. She retrieved it from her purse, then flashed Rennen an apologetic smile. "Sorry, I need to get this."

"No worries."

She slid her finger over the glass to answer. "Hello?" Her face fell as she paced back and forth. "What? Are you okay?" Her hand raked through her hair. "I knew that idiot was trouble," she muttered, her features tightening. "Mami, calm down. I can't understand a word you're saying. Stay right there, and I'll come and get you. Text me the address." She ended the call, shaking her head. "I'm sorry, but I have to go."

"What's wrong?"

She let out a long sigh, shoving her phone in her purse and slipping the strap over her shoulder. "My sobrina Anna."

"Sobrina?" he asked.

"My niece. She's sixteen. Her boyfriend took her to a party with drinking, drugs, and everything else you can imagine. She told him to take her home, but the jerk won't." She threw up her hands, a hard astonishment overtaking her. "He's getting soused and she's standing outside by the curb and needs me to pick her up."

Even as Rennen nodded in understanding, disappointment settled over him. He was nowhere near ready for this night to be over. "I'd like to see you again."

She smiled, shooting a dart of warmth through him. "I'd like that." A hint of teasing trickled into her eyes. "Maybe we can go on that first date."

"Absolutely."

He stepped up to her and ran a finger along the curve of her jaw, appreciating the smooth feel of her olive skin. It took all the fortitude he could muster to keep from pulling her into his arms and kissing her again. "Have dinner with me tomorrow night."

"Sorry, I can't. I'm getting together with my family."

His heart dropped.

"How about Saturday night instead?"

He brightened. For a second there, he feared she might be trying to put him off. "Perfect." They exchanged numbers, and then Ariana lifted her face to his and gave him a peck on the lips. "See you Saturday," she promised as she hurried to her truck.

Rennen watched her walk away, exhilaration and dread warring in his gut. He could still feel Ariana's lips against his. The tangy scent of her fruity shampoo lingered on his senses. To have found someone like her was heaven. Knowing it would all end the moment she learned his identity was a cruel joke. His only chance was to keep the charade going long enough for Ariana to become invested in him before she discovered the truth.

3

Dinners with the family were something Ariana always looked forward to. It was especially fun now that Ace's wife Silver and her daughter Gracie were part of the family.

They all gathered around a large table in a private area of her parent's Mexican restaurant, Los Tios. The fact that Ariana's mother Fabiana would break away from running the restaurant during the dinner shift and leave someone else in charge spoke to the importance of family gatherings.

Ariana glanced at the spread of food, which included steaming platters of beef and chicken fajitas, tamales, enchiladas, beans, rice, and fresh tortillas. She dipped a chip in a bowl of salsa and took a large bite, then turned her attention back to her phone in her lap. Her mother was always getting onto Ariana's brothers for bringing their phones to the table. Fabiana wouldn't be too pleased if she realized Ariana was texting. Ariana knew she should put the phone away, but she and Rennen had been texting back and forth all day long, and she didn't want to break the cycle. Just thinking about their kiss the night before sent heat rushing up her neck. She'd never kissed a guy she'd just met, but Rennen was different—spontaneous and wonderful. She'd discovered today that like her, he loved the outdoors and was game for adventure sports like rock climbing, rafting, and back-packing. Her fingers tapped away sending him another text.

What's on the docket for tomorrow's date?

She kept the phone in her lap while she reached for a tortilla and began filling her plate with fajita meat. Then she scooped out generous portions of rice and beans. She'd taught an extra cardio class today to help offset the massive amount of carbs she knew she'd ingest tonight. Her mom's cooking was legendary. Ariana intended to eat her fill and take some leftovers home for the weekend. She took a large bite of her fajita, the tender steak practically melting in her mouth. Then she took a bite of beans, followed by rice. *Heaven.* As she waited for Rennen's response, she picked up bits of the conversations taking place around her.

"When's your next doctor's appointment?" Fabiana asked Silver.

"This coming Tuesday."

"Oh, hija. That is so wonderful," Fabiana gushed, her expression radiating joy. "I can't wait to find out what you're having."

"A sister," Gracie cheered, holding up a forkful of food like it was a torch.

Ace gave Gracie a tender look. "You never know. It might be a boy. We'll have to wait and see when your mom has the ultrasound."

Gracie's face crumpled into a frown. "No, a sister." She plopped down her fork where it pinged against the plate. Then she crossed her arms over her chest and thrust out her lower lip.

Silver was sitting beside Gracie. She patted her arm. "Remember? We talked about this. You'll love having a brother or a sister."

Gracie let out a long sigh. "Fine."

Ariana couldn't help but smile. Gracie was so darn cute with her blonde pigtails flanked with red ribbons. Gracie was Silver's daughter from a previous marriage, but Ace loved her like his own child. The baby Silver was carrying would be her and Ace's first child together. Used to getting all the attention, Ariana was sure Gracie would be in for a rough adjustment when the baby was born, especially considering Gracie had Down syndrome and found transitions difficult. Still, she was such a sweet little girl and would make a wonderful big sister.

"If it's a girl, I'll have to book Channing Gardens for her Quinceañera," Fabiana said. "Maria Perez told me they're booking up years in advance. As soon as you find out the sex, let me know."

"W-what?" Ace sputtered, glancing at Silver who looked just as surprised. He chuckled out a nervous laugh. "Mom, the baby hasn't even been born yet, and you're planning her Quinceañera. Let's take things one step at a time."

Her younger brother Antonio grinned. "Be careful. She'll have the baby's husband picked out by the time she's three," he said in between bites.

"Now, son, be nice to your mom," Raúl, Ariana's father, said, but there was a glint of amusement in his eyes.

Antonio hooted. "It's true." He pointed, his finger sweeping over Ace and Ariana. You know I'm right. You're just too chicken to say it. "Bok, bok," he clucked, flapping his arms like wings.

Everyone at the table knew Antonio was right, and they all looked at each other, silent laughter passing between them, but no one was going to agree out loud.

Fabiana leaned over to swipe the back of Antonio's head. "Don't talk with your mouth full, hijo," she warned.

Antonio ducked out of her reach. "Hey, now. Don't mess up my hair."

"Mess it up?" Ariana chuckled. "That hair wouldn't move in a hurricane, not with the amount of pomade you've got slathered on it."

Antonio ran a hand along his hair. "You're just jealous, sis. I'll have you know that I was told I have perfect hair the other day."

Ariana lifted an eyebrow. "Is that so? Which girl was that? One of your many admirers?" A smile quivered at the corners of her lips when his cheeks flushed. It was fun to tease her little brother. He'd gone from gangly awkward to a ladies' man in what seemed like a blink of an eye.

Axel wrinkled his nose. "Girls are disgusting," he muttered.

"You keep thinking that for a good long time," Fabiana said. She eyed Antonio. "Who are all these girls Ariana mentioned? And why haven't I met any of them?"

Antonio raised his hands in the air, shooting Ariana an irritated look. "See what you've done?"

Ariana just laughed. "If you're old enough to date, you're old enough to handle Mom." She held up a hand. "Just saying."

"I don't think anyone needs to handle me," Fabiana huffed, sitting up straight and adjusting her dress. She zoned in on Ariana. "Speaking of dating, you haven't brought Paul around lately."

Dang it! She should've seen this one coming. "Mom, I told you. Paul and I aren't together anymore." She glanced at Antonio who gave her a vindicated smile. She could read his thoughts as clearly as if he were yelling them. *Your turn.*

Fabiana frowned. "I really liked Paul."

"Yeah, he's a great guy," Ariana said dully.

"You should bring him around. I miss seeing him."

Ariana groaned. "Mom, would you give it a rest?"

"What? I can't worry about my children?" Fabiana countered. "I want you to find someone and settle down, like Ace did." Fabiana gave Silver a radiant smile.

Ariana looked across the table at Ace who shot her a sympathetic look. When Ace was single, the focus had been on him. But now that he was with Silver, the pressure was on Ariana. Her mother meant well, but she could be overbearing at times.

"Mom, Ariana will settle down when she finds the right guy," Ace said. "Give her some space."

"Thank you," Ariana mouthed.

He smiled and winked.

Gracie tugged on Silver's sleeve. "I want fried ice cream."

Fabiana turned to Axel. "Would you take Gracie to the kitchen and have José make her some ice cream?"

Axel scooted back his chair. He waved a hand. "Sure. Come on, Gracie."

"Make sure to keep a close eye on her," Fabiana warned.

"I hold Axel's hand, Nana" Gracie said. "Then I won't get lost."

Fabiana's features softened as she smiled. "That's a good girl." Fabiana turned to Ace. "So, hijo, what's the latest on the restaurant expansion?"

The air tensed as all eyes turned to Ace. Silver reached for his hand. The small gesture spoke volumes about their relationship and how Silver was always in Ace's corner, backing him up. All of them understood that Fabiana's question about the expansion was really more about how Ace was faring now that the coach had cut him loose from the Titans. The news had broken a month ago, and the media was having a heyday with it. Ariana was glad they were getting it out in the open. They'd been tiptoeing around the topic for weeks. Ace was trying to put on a tough face, but Ariana could tell he was torn up about it. During the thirteenth game of the previous season, Ace had gotten injured with a torn MCL. He went through surgery and months of rehab for his knee and felt he was recovering well. Then the Titans hit him with a whammy, renegotiating his contract to pay him less money for the next season. Ace was frustrated with the situation, but decided to continue playing, saying he'd give it one more year and then retire so the Triple Threat could stay together and get their championship rings. Then he reinjured his knee at the beginning of the off-season team activities, putting him out for good. Ace had always wanted their parents to turn Los Tios into a chain, but Silver was the one taking the ball and running with it, probably to keep Ace's mind occupied.

"We're meeting with a commercial real estate broker next week to scout out locations for restaurants," Ace began. "Our plan is to start with five restaurants in the Metroplex next year. Once those are hopping we'll expand to other cities in Texas."

"Eventually, we'd like to franchise." Silver touched her stomach, a matronly smile touching her lips. "Of course, we'll have to take things a little slow with this one on the way."

Ace put an arm around Silver. "But not too slow, right hon?" A strained smile stretched over his lips. "Silver's trying to keep me preoccupied, so I won't spend so much time brooding over the Titans."

Antonio scowled. "If you ask me, the Titans are making a huge mistake by letting you go. Everything keeps saying how this Ghost guy's gonna come in and save the day, but I don't believe it. He can't be a tenth as good as you."

A wave of tenderness washed over Ariana when she saw the adoration shining on Antonio's face. Ace was his hero. She, of course, agreed one hundred percent with Antonio. Whoever this guy was, he couldn't be as talented and fast as Ace. The guy in question had started out as the Titan's second-string running back. He stepped into the top running back position last season when Ace was injured and was quickly making a name for himself. He'd been dubbed "the Ghost" by the media because he ran so fast he glided. Ariana suspected it was because of this hotshot that the Titans were so anxious to cut Ace loose. While her head knew Ace being replaced was a natural part of the NFL process, her heart ached over the pain it caused her brother. In fact, she never would've agreed to do the youth camp the following day if she'd known how the Titans were going to treat Ace. She'd committed to teach agility classes months ago when Ace was on the team. Oh, well, there was no getting out of it now. And it wasn't the kids' fault the Titan coach was a jerk. "I agree with Antonio. This Ghost doesn't hold a candle to you."

Ariana's phone vibrated. She glanced down. Rennen was answering her question about plans for their date tomorrow night.

I don't want to give away the surprise. But rest assured it'll blow your mind.

She smiled as she typed back.

You might be surprised. It takes a lot to blow this girl's mind.

He responded,

I'll see what I can do. But first, I've got to get Red all spit-shined and ready to go.

Maybe I should just let the two of you go out. After all, three's a crowd.

He sent her a line of emojis making various faces.

Ariana had to admit, Rennen was impressive. A smile curved her lips. She couldn't wait for their date. It was then that she realized all eyes were on her. She looked up, her face warming. "What?"

Ace pointed. "We were wondering what is so important."

"I recognize that smile," Silver added. "Must be a guy."

"Paul?" Fabiana asked, hope coating her voice.

Ariana tightened her grip on her phone. "No, Mom, it's not Paul."

"Oh, so it *is* a guy," Ace said, a teasing light flickering in his eyes. "What's his name? Do I know him?"

She laughed. "No, you don't know him." She rolled her eyes. "Ace thinks he knows everyone."

"You might be surprised at the people I know. What's his name?" Ace pressed.

Fabiana leaned forward. "Is it getting serious?"

"No, Mom. I just met him last night. We're going on our first date tomorrow."

Antonio put his arm to his mouth, making smooching sounds. "Now who's the one with the admirer?"

She stuck out her tongue.

"Tell us about him," Silver said. "What does he do for a living?"

Ariana cocked her head. "You know, I don't even know." She would've found out had the evening not been cut short by Anna's fiasco. Luckily, she'd been able to get Anna home safe and sound. Her aunt and uncle thanked her profusely for coming to Anna's aid, but Ariana told them thanks wasn't necessary—that's what families did … helped each other.

Ace made a face. "How did you meet this guy?"

"We sang karaoke together." She left it at that, not wanting to bring up meeting at a club. Her mother would freak.

Ace pumped his eyebrows. "Karaoke, huh? What's his name?" When she remained silent, he spread his hands, a sly smile spreading over his lips. "You know we're gonna keep pressing you until you tell us. Oh, and you'd better go ahead and invite him over so we can meet him. Otherwise, Mom won't rest a wink."

"That's right," Fabiana nodded, the skin underneath her chin jiggling as she set her jaw in a firm stance. She put a hand on Raúl's arm. "You want to meet him too, don't you?"

Raúl nodded. "Yes, eventually, if things progress to the next level after they go out."

Fabiana waved away the comment. "Of course it'll work out. Why wouldn't it?" She looked at Ariana. "Is he a good guy?"

Ariana fought the urge to roll her eyes. No matter how old she was, her mom treated her like she was ten. "Yeah, he's great."

"You should call him up and invite him over tonight. We have plenty of food," Fabiana said, an eager light shining in her eyes.

"I'm not gonna invite him over tonight, Mom." *Sheesh.* That was the downside of having a close family, everybody in your business 24/7. She sighed. "If you must know, his name's Rennen Bradley. Like I said, we haven't even gone out on our first date." She looked at her mom. "So it's a little early to start picking out my wedding dress."

Ace's eyes bulged as he made a gurgling sound. "What did you say?"

Ariana tensed. "Rennen Bradley."

"What does he look like?"

Ariana's heart hammered in her chest. What in the heck was going on? Ace's face had gone purple. "About six feet tall with blonde, curly hair."

"I don't believe this." Ace let out a humorless laugh, bringing his fist to his mouth.

Alarm trickled down Ariana's spine. "What?" she demanded.

"He's the Ghost," Ace blurted, a wild look in his eyes.

Ariana sucked in a breath, her hands starting to shake.

"Rennen Bradley is the running back who replaced me."

The hurt in Ace's eyes cut her to the core, making her feel like the biggest traitor on the planet. "I—I had no idea." This was bad. Really bad. Ariana clicked through the events from last night. How Rennen had looked so surprised when he learned she was Ace's sister. Rennen must've been laughing inside when she gave him the spiel about not gushing over Ace. A splitting pain shot across her forehead as she clutched her napkin in her fist. He'd played her. How could he not have told her who he was? A stunned silence came over the room with everyone staring at her. Suddenly, it was too much. She had to get away to process this. Tears burned her eyes. Not hurt tears, but fighting mad tears that she'd let her guard down, had let herself believe for a few charmed hours that Rennen might be the real deal —the guy she'd been searching for. "Excuse me," she mumbled as she got up from the table and rushed out of the room.

4

He'd known it was coming, the dread lodged in the back of his mind the entire day. Rennen had hoped he could tell Ariana who he was in person before she found out from someone else. He should've told her last night when he first learned she was Ace's sister. Then again, if he had, she would've ended it then and there.

He'd received one line from her.

I know who you are.

He tried to call her to explain why he'd held back, but she didn't answer. After five more calls, leaving messages on her voicemail each time, it was apparent she wasn't going to answer. So he sent her a text.

I was just as shocked as you when I found out you were Ace's sister. I would've told you last night, but you rushed off to take care of your niece. I was planning on telling you in person first thing tomorrow.

He waited on pins and needs for her response. His heart lurched when it came through.

Don't ever contact me again.

He swallowed, his mind not wanting to admit that this relationship with Ariana was over before it even had a chance to begin. A quiet desperation seeped over him as the all-too-familiar feelings of rejection reared their ugly head. "The irony," he muttered. The odds of running into Ace's sister in the Dallas/Ft. Worth Metroplex with seven million people had to be slim to none. And yet, he had. Maybe he should just forget about her and channel his energy into his career. He balled his fist. Who was he kidding? He'd been able to think of little else other than Ariana ever since he met her.

It was insane to think that a woman he'd only met once—and kissed—could have such a strong effect on him. It probably wouldn't take much to track down her gym. The worst that could happen was that she might throw him out ... or lay him out like she did the football coach. A smile stole over his lips. He'd risk it, if it meant seeing her again. Tomorrow was Saturday. He wondered if she worked weekends. Probably not. But still, he could find the gym and scope things out. Dang it! No, he couldn't do that. He had another commitment tomorrow. Okay, he'd go Monday after he got through with his training session, which would be over by lunchtime.

His phone buzzed. For one wild second, he thought it might be Ariana, but it was his agent. "Hey, Monroe," he said, swallowing his disappointment.

"Hey. You are on fire, my man. Lighting up the channels. Everybody wants to know more about 'the Ghost' that busted up the Triple Threat and replaced Ace Sanchez."

Rennen winced, the sting of Ariana's text hitting him like a punch in the gut. "It wasn't my fault that Ace got injured."

"No, it was nobody's fault. These things happen. But you're the lucky man who happened to be waiting in the wings, ready to take over." He let out a deviant chuckle. "And take over you did."

"Luck had nothing to do with it. I've worked my tail off to get where I am," he shot back.

Monroe let out an easy laugh. "I hear ya, man. You're testier than a cornered goat. What's crawled up your jockey shorts?"

He blew out a breath. "Sorry, it's been a rough night."

"What's going on?"

Rennen raked a hand through his hair. "I'd rather not go into it, if you don't mind."

Long pause. "Just remember that I'm here for you, if you need to talk."

"Thanks, man. I appreciate it," he added, feeling guilty for taking out his frustration on Monroe. A black guy from Seattle Washington, Monroe was a rock star agent in the sports arena, and Rennen was lucky to have him in his corner. Monroe only represented top players, one of his most notable being the legendary Rigby "Rocket" Breeland. Rennen felt honored that Monroe considered him a high enough caliber player to represent him. And it was partly due to Monroe's hard-nosed negotiating skills that the Titans were paying Rennen such a large amount.

Monroe became all business. "Anyway, the reason I'm calling on a Friday night is because I've got some great news."

"I could use some good news." He brightened a little at the prospect.

"Katie Moss from the CBS primetime show *Up Close* has agreed to an exclusive interview with you this coming Tuesday afternoon. The DaVinci Firm set everything up. Katie wants to do the interview in your home, so viewers can get an in-depth look at your life."

"Uh, really?" Rennen's stomach tensed. He glanced around his condo. He didn't want Katie Moss coming into his personal space and broadcasting it to the world. "Maybe we should pick another location."

"Don't worry. They'll only film in one small section of your living room."

"I don't know man. That feels too personal."

"That's the idea ... and the only way Katie would agree to the interview." When Rennen remained silent, Monroe rushed to speak. "It's like we talked about. This interview will help you set the record straight about your past and dispel all these salacious stories that keep cropping up." He chuckled. "You're on the fast-track, dude. And with a background like yours, everyone's dying to know the full story. The trick is to spin the story the way you want, use it to your advantage."

Deep down, Rennen knew Monroe was right. Ever since the news broke a few weeks ago that the Titans had signed a two-year contract for 12.3 million with Rennen for the starting running back position, reporters came crawling out the woodwork, wanting interviews. It didn't take long for them to drag up the details of his past, growing up in foster homes, never knowing who his real parents were. Phrases like *foster care survivor* and *rags-to-riches* were being thrown around. Rennen could handle just about anything the press threw at him, but what he couldn't handle was the scores of people claiming to be his parents.

It disgusted him how so many people wanted to cling to his coat-tails now that he was somebody. Where were his parents when he was a defenseless kid? What kind of mother would desert her baby? These were the questions that had plagued him his entire life, still plagued him. When the press started hounding Rennen, Monroe suggested that Rennen hire a PR firm to be his voice and help field the reporters. Rennen hired The DaVinici Firm, a local group who represented other Titan players, including starting quarterback Kade Kincaid. The firm was known for helping clients spin a positive light on potentially damaging situations.

"All right," Rennen finally said. "Let's do it."

"Awesome. Lainey Summerfield from the DaVinci Firm will contact you with all the details."

"Sounds good." Rennen met Lainey the week prior. She was his point of contact at DaVinci. In her mid-fifties, Lainey was approachable and seemed to know her stuff. It would be good to have her as a buffer between him and the press.

"And you're doing the Tiny Titans Football Camp tomorrow, right?"

"Right."

"Good, events like that can only help."

Unlike Monroe, Rennen hadn't viewed the camp as a PR opportunity but was more concerned about giving back to the community, spending time with at-risk kids. Now, he kind of wished he hadn't committed to it because it would take up the bulk of his day, meaning that he had to put off trying to find Ariana's gym. Monroe went through a long list of pointers, things Rennen should say to the press. Halfway listening, his thoughts went back to Ariana. If only she'd give him a chance to talk to her in person, he was sure they could work things out. She seemed like a reasonable person.

Ace had a great career, longer than most running backs in the NFL. But someone was bound to replace him eventually. The same would happen with Rennen, which is why Monroe fought so hard to get him a sizable contract for the next two years. If Rennen weren't taking Ace's place, someone else would.

He smiled, thinking about Ariana's spunk. Her dark eyes were filled with enough vitality for ten lifetimes. She was tough, yet feminine with her subtle curves. He kept thinking about how her stilettos showcased her shapely legs and her wispy hair framed her exotic face. The excitement he felt around her was intoxicating.

When Rennen first started playing football in high school, it felt like he was restoring a part of himself. For the first time in his life, he was the best at something. Football seeped into his blood, and he knew he could never let it go. As crazy as it was, he was having some of those same feelings about Ariana. Now that he'd met her, he didn't want to let her go. But that was ridiculous. They'd spent a couple meager hours together at a club. Yeah, the kiss had been spectacular, but it was one kiss. He couldn't help but laugh at himself. Maybe all the stress from the press was starting to get to him. Then again, he couldn't shake the feeling that he was supposed to meet Ariana.

"Hey man," Monroe said. "I'm getting another call. Can you hold a minute?"

"Sure," Rennen said absently, his thoughts rambling. When Rennen was in high school, he'd channeled his energy into the one thing that had never failed him—football. His desire to be the best carried him through college on a full ride at Ohio State. He was drafted to play for the Sacramento Vipers in the seventh round and was later traded to the Titans, which Rennen was ecstatic about because it got him back to Texas and gave him the opportunity to play back-up to the great Ace Sanchez. As soon as Rennen achieved one goal, he'd push through to another. His ultimate goal was to secure a lucrative contract as a starter. He assumed when he reached that point, he'd finally feel complete. But a strange thing happened. Now that Rennen had gotten everything he thought he always wanted, he felt more lost than ever. For some time, he'd been praying for clarity to be able to understand what he was feeling.

When he was a kid, he kept a running prayer in his heart that he'd find his mom. But as time went on, and the prayer remained unanswered, he became angry at God. During junior high and his freshman year of high school, he was headed down a dark path that might've destroyed him had the Boyd family not entered his life. At the time, Rennen was living with a foster family, the Youngs, an elderly couple with no children of their own. For the Youngs, foster care was a business. While Howard and Denise Young kept Rennen at a distance emotionally, his physical needs were met, which was a drastic improvement over previous situations Rennen had been in. Rennen had mastered putting up a good front to the Youngs, while getting into drugs and alcohol.

It was during this time that Rennen met Warren Boyd when they had a science class together. Warren was a popular kid whose dad Gary was the high school track coach. For some reason, Warren took an interest in Rennen. They eventually became friends, mostly because Warren wouldn't have it any other way. Rennen joined the track team and Gary recognized his potential. Rennen became a track star and then transitioned into football.

Things took a downward turn, however, when Rennen's foster father, Howard, died of cancer. His wife Denise had a mental breakdown and could no longer care for herself, much less Rennen. Rennen would've been moved to another town with a different set of foster parents had the Boyds not stepped in. They worked it out through the state so Rennen could live with them the remainder of his high school career.

The three years Rennen spent with the Boyds were the happiest in his life. For the first time, Rennen got a taste of what it was like to be part of a real family. Rennen had coped with his turbulent past the best way he knew how. He thought he'd put the worst of it behind him until news of his contract with the Titans went public, and people started coming forward claiming to be his parents. Anger surged through him as he clenched his fist. He just wanted his past to stay in the past where it belonged.

The night before, Rennen had been pretty low when Doug and Matt, fellow Titan players, stopped by and invited him to a karaoke club. Rennen told them *no* at first, but they kept after him, saying he was too keyed up and needed to release a little steam. He was digging his heels in to refuse, but then had a strong feeling that he needed to go. When he got to the club and started dancing, it felt good to let loose and simply enjoy the moment. Then he met Ariana and assumed that was why he needed to go. Seeing how things had fallen apart with her, Rennen didn't know what to make of his feelings. He rubbed a hand across his forehead. Maybe he was making too much of this. A good night's sleep would help him view things more clearly. Ariana was one girl, after all. Rennen had tons of girls lining up to date him. It wasn't smart to get hung up on the one who got away. Thoughts of her flooded him again. He could almost smell her fruity shampoo, feel her in his arms.

"You there, man?" Monroe asked.

"Yeah, I'm still here."

"Sorry that call took so long."

"No problem."

They spoke a few more minutes about the upcoming interview and camp the following day. They ended the call and Rennen rubbed his hand over his face. He needed a good night's sleep to help recharge his battery. Tomorrow, he'd forget about Ariana and focus on his career. As much as he wanted to, he wouldn't go searching for her gym.

Relationships were complicated enough without adding the extra layer of her being Ace's sister. He went to the fridge to grab a water. He lifted the bottle to his lips and drained it in a few swigs, then crushed it in one hand and tossed it in the nearby garbage bin.

He couldn't resist the temptation to look at his texts to see if Ariana had responded while he was talking to Monroe. Disappointment stabbed through him. She hadn't. He grunted. Of course not. She'd told him to never contact her again. It didn't get any clearer than that.

"Forget her," he muttered. "Don't be stupid. You don't need any more drama in your life."

He needed sleep. Heck, he might even call up a few girls to arrange dates for the next few weeks. That would help take his mind off Ariana. He straightened his shoulders, feeling a little better now that he'd worked out a plan. Plans were good, giving him something concrete to work towards. He'd do as he'd always done, put one foot in front of the other and move forward until his feelings got in line with his head. Yes, that was the sensible thing to do. In a couple of weeks, Ariana would be a distant memory.

Onto bigger and better things.

5

Despite her frustration with the Titans for letting Ace go, Ariana was suddenly glad she'd agreed to teach the agility portion of the first-annual Tiny Titans Football Camp as she looked at the eager expressions of the fresh-faced boys surrounding her. They were on a section of the practice field in the state-of-the art Titan complex that included the game stadium, a workout center, and executive offices on the upper floors. Cedar Bell the intern over the camp had planned everything to a T, which was nice because it allowed Ariana to focus on the boys.

"Are you ready to have some fun?" she yelled.

"Yeah!" they responded.

"My name is Ariana. I want you to tell me your names." She pursed her lips together. "Let's see ... how can we make this more interesting?" She held up finger. "I know, also tell me your favorite player."

The boys jabbered excitedly amongst themselves. She'd known this would capture their interest. Thanks to Antonio and Axel, Ariana knew how to relate to boys. Now, if she'd been asked to teach a class to a group of girls, it would've been a different story. Boys were easy.

Just give them plenty of physical activity, sprinkle in a little competition, and feed them lots of snacks and they'd be happy.

They went down the line, telling their names and favorite players. It was gratifying to hear a couple of them name Ace. Of course, next year, they'd be chanting Rennen Bradley's name instead. Irritation squelched over Ariana as the protective sister in her came out full force. She kept replaying the stunned look on Ace's face when he realized the guy Ariana was talking about was his replacement on the Titan team.

Regret pressed heavily on her chest as she thought of Rennen Bradley. She'd been flying so high after meeting him that the crash back to earth was rough. After she learned who he was, she'd Googled him. There were so many crazy stories about Rennen's past it was hard to know what was fact and what was fiction. One online magazine claimed he was raised by a group of ranchers. Another, notorious for stretching the truth, said Rennen was a test-tube baby. From what Ariana could piece together, Rennen had been abandoned as a baby, then passed around various foster homes. According to one article from a more reputable source, Rennen had been removed from one home as a baby due to cigarette burns and unexplained bruises on his little body. Realizing this about him made her heart hurt. She felt guilty for the harsh texts she'd sent. Then again, her loyalty was to Ace. Despite Rennen's upbringing, he was taking Ace's spot. And that meant there could never be anything between them. She pulled her thoughts back to the task at hand.

She lifted the whistle hanging by a string around her neck. "I need you to form two lines. Make sure you're an arm's width apart. Every athlete needs to be in top-notch condition to perform well on the field."

"Where's the football?" a freckle-faced boy with glasses asked.

"There's much more to football than merely the ball," Ariana countered. "Before you even think about passing that ball, you've got to get a good grasp of what your feet are doing."

"You can practice most of these drills at home. I suggest doing them three or four days a week. When I blow the whistle, you're going to jog in place, get your knees as high as you can. Use your hands to propel your legs up. Like so." She demonstrated it. "We'll start slower and then build up speed. Follow my lead. Ready, go."

She blew the whistle and jogged in place. The boys copied her movements. The idea was to take them through a few simple drills and add in games to make it interesting. She'd put together an obstacle course where two groups could compete relay style. The Kincaid brothers would pop-in the last ten to fifteen minutes of the segment and work with the boys on a few fundamentals. And much to the boys' delight, they'd show them how to throw a football.

They jogged for about three minutes until Ariana blew the whistle for them to stop. The boy with freckles and another boy were sucking air and clutching their stomachs like they'd just run a marathon.

"You trying to kill us, lady?" the freckle-faced boy grumbled.

Ariana bit back a smile. He was so darn cute, but she could tell from the deviant look in his eyes that he was a handful. There was normally at least one heckler in every group. Heck, she couldn't say much because she'd been that heckler when she was the kid's age. "Nope," she said pleasantly. "Just trying to teach you a few things to help you get in good shape."

Most of the boys had come here with stars in their eyes, wanting to meet famous football players. All one hundred spots were filled almost as fast as the slots opened. Ariana was sure being put through tough drills by a girl was a letdown. She'd need to take it slow so she wouldn't tire them out too soon. And she'd have to make sure they drank plenty of water on breaks. She looked at the boy. "What did you say your name was?"

"Chris," he said hesitantly.

"All right, Chris ..." her eyes moved over the group "... and all the rest of you. Let me show you a few more drills." Ariana made sure to add stretching and breathing exercises in between. After they were sufficiently warmed up, she pointed to two rope ladders spread across the AstroTurf, parallel to each other. "I want you to take turns running through the ladders, making sure the balls of your feet touch every space in between the rungs. Keep your knees high like we did before and use your hands to propel forward. Keep your steps light. Like so." She ran through the ladder. "Okay, your turn."

Chris let out an exaggerated sigh. The heavyset kid standing next to him did the same. "Do we have to do it?"

Ariana kept her tone neutral. "You can run laps around the field instead, if you want."

They went bug-eyed. "No," Chris said. "We're good."

She grinned. "Thought so."

After they got the hang of it, she motioned for them to gather around her. "Now, for the fun part." She flashed an exuberant smile and was pleased when most of them smiled back, anticipation brimming in their eyes. "I want you to call off one and two as I point to you." She ran through the group. "The *ones* gather on my right, the *twos* on my left."

She pointed at the obstacle course. "Here's what we're gonna do. You'll go through the ladder first, then the cones, and zigzag through the markers, making sure to touch each one. After you finish the course, run back and tag the hand of your teammate who'll then go through the course. The first group through wins an extra snack." She pumped her eyebrows. "And I've got something really tasty."

"What is it?" a tow-haired boy asked, eagerness lighting his eyes.

"You'll have to wait and find out." She rubbed her hands together. "Huddle up. Everyone put an arm in and on the count of three, we'll yell 'Titans'. Ready?" They piled their hands over hers. "One, two, three. Titans!" they boomed.

Ariana motioned. "All right. Line up, boys. A little competition's good for the soul."

"I couldn't agree more." Her breath caught as she turned toward the voice and found herself staring into a familiar set of green eyes flecked with gold. A lock of his hair fell over one eye, giving him a sexy-windswept look. He was wearing a sleeveless t-shirt and athletic shorts, offering a bird's-eye view of his defined biceps and muscular legs. Her heart picked up a notch. "Rennen, what're you doing here?"

"I was told to come over and help with the agility exercises. Make sure you're teaching them correct form."

The comment set her off like a spark to dry grass, igniting a raging fire. Ariana straightened to her full height, her hands going to her hips. "Who told you to come over here?" She was volunteering her time to do this, and was perfectly capable of teaching a group of kids agility drills. She craned her neck looking for Cedar and found her near the water station holding a baby on her hip while pressing the button to fill a camper's cup.

Amusement sparkled in his eyes. "That's not important."

Ariana scrunched her brows. "Well, it's important to me." It took her half a second to realize he was baiting her. As she drove to camp this morning, she'd briefly wondered if Rennen might be here. She'd mentally prepared herself to act aloof so he'd get the message loud and clear that she wasn't interested. But when she didn't see him, she assumed she was in the clear. Obviously not.

He motioned. "An obstacle course, huh?"

"We're doing relay races," one of the boys explained.

"And the winning team gets an extra snack," another added.

Rennen folded his arms over his chest, his tone musing. "Interesting." He looked at the boys. "What do you say, we raise the stakes?"

"Yeah," they chimed.

Ariana tensed. She didn't know what Rennen was up to, but it couldn't be good. "We've already got our plan." She jutted out her chin. If Rennen thought he could come out here and switch up everything on a whim, he'd be sorely disappointed.

"I'll join one of the groups. You join the other."

"No," she balked. "This isn't about us. This is about the boys." She stepped closer to him, lowering her voice. "I'm sorry about what happened between us, Rennen. But let's not drag these boys into it."

His eyes hardened as he chuckled. "Really? You're sorry? You could've fooled me. You lambasted me with those texts. And then wouldn't answer my calls."

Ariana glanced at the boys who were hanging on every word. "Let's not do this here."

Rennen cocked an eyebrow. "If we hadn't run into each other today, you never would've spoken to me again."

That was true. She just looked at him. "So?"

"So, you're being totally unfair."

A harsh laugh rose in her throat as she pointed to her chest. "Me?" She shot him a condemning look. "You should've told me who you were when we first met."

"I was working my way towards it when you had to leave to pick up your niece."

She shook her head. "I don't buy that. You could've told me earlier."

He cocked an eyebrow. "When? In the middle of your rant about how much you hate football players?"

"You hate football players?" one of the boys asked, a perplexed look on his face.

Heat rushed up her neck. "Thanks a lot," she muttered, jerking her chin towards the kids.

He held up his hands. "I'm just stating what happened. If I had told you who I was at the beginning, would you have been more understanding?"

She rocked back. "Well, no."

A vindicated look swept over him. "I understand you being upset, but it's not my fault Ace got injured. That's the nature of the game. If I weren't taking his place, someone else would. You don't have to crucify me for it."

The skin on the back of her neck prickled like it was crawling with ants. She squared her jaw. "That may be true, but I sure as heck don't have to date you." The words came out hoarse as they stood, eyeing each other.

"Okay, let's make a wager. Like I said earlier, I'll join one team. You join the other. If your team wins, I'll honor your wish and leave you alone."

She shook her head. "This is ridiculous. I can't believe you're doing this now, in the middle of camp."

He continued. "If I win, you'll go out on a date with me." He held up a finger. "One date is all I ask."

She let out a strangled laugh. "What? You're insane! There's no way I'm going on a date with you."

A cocky smile tugged at his lips. "Are you so sure you're gonna lose?"

She rubbed her chin. If he weren't so dang good looking, it might be easier to resist him. No, she couldn't think such thoughts. She had to be strong. "Hmm ... let me think about this. The Ghost challenges me to an obstacle race and I'm just supposed to accept? That's a little like a fish challenging a squirrel to a swim, isn't it?" She twirled her hand. "Let's see ... no thanks." Her jaw tightened as she shot him a look that could stop an army in its tracks. "Despite what you think, I'm not stupid."

His eyes held hers. For a moment, she forgot about the group of boys surrounding them. "I never thought you were," he said softly.

"You're the Ghost?" Chris asked, wide-eyed. He looked at the other boys. "Holy smokes. It's the Ghost everyone's been talking about."

"Yep, he's the superstar," Ariana piped in, not trying to hide her resentment.

"Can I get your autograph?" a boy asked.

"Or a selfie," another said.

Ariana glared at them. "No, you may not. Not until after our class is over."

"Okay, you make a good point about the race," Rennen said. "We'll pick something else."

A laugh escaped her lips. "You don't give up, do you?"

"Never."

The word was spoken so fiercely that it sent a jolt through her. *Geez.* This guy was messing with her head. Her eyes seemed to have a mind of their own as they went to his lips. Desire swelled through her, making her feel hot all over.

"You pick the activity. Just me and you."

Her heart hammered in her chest as her mouth went dry. "Here? No way."

A quirky expression came over his handsome face, as his voice took on a taunting edge. "Is Ace so fragile that he has to get his big sister to fight his battles? What a cry-baby," he smirked.

Ariana gritted her teeth. "Ace's younger sister, actually."

His mouth twitched. "Oops, sorry."

She wanted to knock the smirk off his lips. He was standing there all smug like he was king of the world. "All right, Goldie Locks, it's on. Hand-to-hand combat." She felt a burst of triumph when she saw the flicker of surprise in his eyes. He was in over his head now. She was gonna eat his lunch.

A broad smile spread over his lips. "Let's do it."

"Fight, fight," the boys chanted with pumped fists.

"It's not a fight," Ariana corrected, "but a sparring match. Back up," she ordered, not wanting any of them to get hurt when Rennen went flying.

Rennen's eyes danced as he crouched down, hands out, ready to take her down. "What're the rules?"

"First one whose back touches the ground loses," she said savagely, planting her feet in a battle stance. Rennen was playing in her world now. "Too bad I have to embarrass you in front of your adoring fans."

He cocked an eyebrow. "Too bad I have to put such a beautiful woman down."

Heat blotched her cheeks. He was probably complimenting her to throw her off. Well, it wouldn't work. She knew all the tricks in the book.

"Nice earrings, by the way." He pointed to her diamond studs. "Looks kind of groovy with your yoga pants and t-shirt. A tough, glamour-girl sort of thing."

Chris wrinkled his nose in disgust. "Are you gonna flirt with her all day or fight?"

Rennen lunged first and tried to grab her arm, but Ariana blocked his attempt with an upward sweep of her arm and darted out of his reach. *Sheesh.* He was fast. It was a good thing she hadn't taken him up on the obstacle course challenge or she'd be toast.

They circled around, each trying to get the upper hand.

She went for him next to sweep his leg with her foot, but he side-stepped her effort. She stumbled, trying to catch her balance. This time, he caught hold of her arm and spun her around, pinning her arm behind her back. He leaned in, his breath tickling her ear. "Do you yield?"

Tingles circled down her spine as a slow-burning desire simmered in her stomach. It was ridiculous how attracted she was to Rennen.

"This is kind of fun," he murmured, his lips grazing her earlobe.

He sounded like he knew exactly how much she was affected by him, which irritated the heck out of her. "Yep, sure is," she growled, digging her heel into bone on top of his foot.

He released his hold, grunting in pain as she whirled around, bringing her knee to his crotch. His eyes widened as he doubled over, his hands moving instinctively to protect himself. While he was inca-pacitated, she swept his leg, sending him spiraling to the ground with a swift thud.

The boys went crazy, jumping up and down, cheering.

Ariana leaned over, peering down at him. "It looks like I just ghosted the Ghost."

He winced. "A knee to the crotch. Really? You don't play fair. There goes any hope for children."

She clucked her tongue. "Now who's the cry-baby?"

He looked up at her with puppy-dog eyes. "Best two out of three?"

She had to hand it to him. He was persistent. In that aspect, he reminded her of Ace. Despite her best effort to hold it back, a smile tugged at her lips. "I don't think so." As their eyes locked, she realized with a bitter disappointment that she wanted him in her life badly. Almost enough to make her kneel and throw her arms around him to rehash their kiss from the other night. Fate was a cruel demon, laughing down at her right now. Why did Rennen have to be the one to take Ace's place? It was so unfair that she had to choose between him and Ace. Of course she'd choose Ace, a hundred times over. And yet, it was so dang hard.

Rennen assessed her with such a compelling look that she could swear he knew what she was thinking. "You know all bets are off, right?"

She jerked. "What're you talking about?"

He sat up, shaking his head. "Like I said, a knee to the crotch isn't fair." He looked at the boys surrounding them. "Am I right?"

"Yeah," a few said hesitantly, not meeting Ariana's eyes.

She didn't know if she should be impressed or annoyed that Rennen was so stinking stubborn. A tendril of hope sprang in her chest at the knowledge that he wasn't giving up. She lifted her chin and adopted an *I couldn't care less attitude* as she pushed her hair behind her ear. "I don't have time to argue about this with you. I've got a class to teach."

She clapped her hands. "Okay, boys. Show's over. Vamanos. You've got an obstacle course to run."

Rennen looked up at her and winked, all the confidence in the world shining in his eyes. "See ya around, slugger."

6

Ariana looked at Beth, the attractive receptionist in her young twenties. Beth worked the front desk of the gym and helped with the office work. She put her hand over the receiver. "It's another reporter."

"Seriously?" Ariana waved a hand, her expression going sour as she turned her attention back to today's schedule. "I'm not here," she muttered.

Beth nodded in understanding.

It had been a busy morning, and the afternoon wasn't going to be any better. When Ariana returned from lunch, she discovered that two instructors had called saying they weren't going to make it in today. She had a back-up she could call to cover the Zumba class at four, but that instructor could only teach one hour. The circuit-training class at two was the problem. Normally Ariana could fill in, but she was teaching a high-intensity cardio class during the same time.

She rubbed a hand across her forehead. They were short-staffed and needed to hire more people, but the funds weren't there. Members of the circuit-training class wouldn't be happy when they showed up today to a cancelled class. She glanced outside, glad to see the reporters had left. A couple were still lurking around when she darted out for a quick lunch. How in the heck was Ariana supposed to run a gym in the middle of all this hoopla?

The phone at the gym had been ringing off the hook for the past three days, mostly reporters wanting a scoop on the story. One of the kids at camp filmed Ariana and Rennen's sparring match with an iPhone and posted it on YouTube. The crazy thing went viral over the weekend and was picking up steam. The caption on the video read, *Ace Sanchez's sister ghosts the Ghost.*

Ariana was mortified when she first saw it. She'd hoped teaching the class at the Tiny Titans Football Camp might generate some publicity for her gym. It had certainly done that, but not in the way she'd hoped. This morning when she arrived to teach a six a.m. kickboxing class, half a dozen reporters were waiting for her. She'd pushed past them repeating "no comment." Ariana was surprised they'd come out so early in the morning. Then again, anything concerning Rennen was high priority. Especially after his live interview with Katie Moss Tuesday evening. Ariana had watched the entire thing with rapt attention.

Rennen's story was similar to the reputable source she'd found online. His first memory was of being in a group home. He'd been with a set of foster parents before that but was removed from the home when the social worker saw cigarette burns and bruises on his arms and legs.

After the group home, Rennen was passed around to a few other foster homes before going to live with the family of his high school friend. Rennen had no knowledge of what happened to his parents. But according to his case file, he was found wandering alone at a bus station—ragged and hungry—and that was how he first came to be in the system. Football had been his saving grace, his ticket to an education and now, his livelihood.

Ariana figured Ace had also watched the interview. She would've liked to have gotten his take on Rennen's background, but wasn't about to bring it up. It was hard not to feel a chord of sympathy for Rennen who'd barreled his way to stardom against all obstacles.

Ariana's family was the most precious thing in the world to her. She couldn't imagine going through life alone.

At one point in the interview, Ariana had choked with emotion. Katie talked about Rennen's nickname and how it was appropriate because he ran so fast that he appeared to be gliding. She asked Rennen what he thought of the nickname. He paused for an entire minute or more before answering. Ariana could feel the tension building in Rennen. Felt herself growing more nervous when she saw him clench his hands.

"For me, the nickname has multiple meanings." Rennen offered a polite smile. "Aside from the obvious running aspect. Growing up without a family was tough. It's primarily through the family that children form their identities. But for me, I never had that." His voice trembled slightly. "I guess I've always felt a little like a ghost, like part of me is missing." He spread his hands. "I suppose all foster children feel that way."

"Why did you agree to do this interview tonight?" Katie asked.

Slight pause. "I wanted to tell my story. Dispel the rumors that have been circulating."

She laughed, glancing at her notes. "Yes, I've read a few zingers. I believe The Daily Sentinel has you being dropped from an alien ship onto the roof of the Alamo."

"Yeah, I kind of like the one that claims I was raised by a pack of wolves." He looked into the camera, a crooked smile tugging at his lips. "Not true."

Ariana had melted a little at that. Even on TV, he was irresistible.

"What do you think about the scores of people coming forward, claiming to be your parents?"

Rennen's jaw hardened. "Well, Katie, forgive me for being blunt, but I think it's a bunch of hogwash."

She rocked back. "Strong words."

"I've been going it alone my whole life and am doing okay. I have no intention of changing things now."

Katie cocked her head, giving him a probing look. "So, you're saying that you don't want to know who your real parents are?"

A tight smile fixed over Rennen's face, causing Ariana's heart to catch. She could feel his pain as if it were her own. His eyes were hard marbles. "That's exactly what I'm saying. Next topic, please."

It took Katie a fraction of a moment to readjust as she thumbed through her notes. "Tell me about this sparring match you had over the weekend with Ariana Sanchez, the sister of Ace Sanchez."

Ariana held her breath, waiting for Rennen's response, her heartbeat roaring like a river in her ears.

Rennen smiled. "She's tough. Obviously."

Katie played the clip for the TV audience. Afterwards, she shook her head, a gleeful expression on her face. "I'm sure this has women everywhere cheering. Tell us about this video."

Rennen squirmed in his seat. "Ariana and I were both helping out at the Tiny Titans Football Camp. What you saw was mostly horsing around."

"Bull crap," Ariana muttered, feeling a burst of pride that she'd taken him down.

Katie leaned forward. "Did this match have anything to do with the fact that you're taking Ace's place on the Titans?"

Rennen flashed an easy smile. "It had more to do with a date."

Her eyes widened. "A date as in a particular day of the month? Or a date, as in courting?" Her expression went coy as she looked at the camera.

"I'll let you figure that out," Rennen said.

"Come on now. Don't leave the viewers hanging." Katie gave him a nervous laugh.

He shook his head. "That's all I have to say about that." His voice was firm, unyielding.

An awkward silence passed. "So, will there be a rematch?"

Rennen looked straight into the camera, his compelling eyes striking Ariana with such force that she felt like he was looking right at her. "I sincerely hope so."

"Um, there's another call for you," Beth said, interrupting Ariana's thoughts.

She arched an eyebrow. "Another reporter?" Or Paul? *Please don't let it be Paul.* Ever since the news of Ariana and Rennen's sparring match had gone viral, her ex-boyfriend Paul had taken a sudden interest in her again. Yesterday, he sent a text asking if she wanted to grab lunch sometime. Even though they'd broken up, they were still on friendly terms. A friendship with Paul was the only thing Ariana wanted. Too bad Paul wasn't getting the hint.

"No, James Knight's personal assistant, Amanda."

Ariana's jaw went slack. "James Knight, the owner of the Titans?"

Beth nodded slowly, wide-eyed.

"What does she want?"

"I don't know." Beth held out the phone. "But I think you should take it."

Ariana's heart lurched. Were they calling to tell her she'd broken some Titan rule by sparring with Rennen on the practice field? Her heart pounded erratically in her chest as she tried to keep her voice even. "Hello?"

"Hello, Ms. Sanchez, this is Amanda Richards, James Knight's personal assistant."

She swallowed. "Yes?"

"I'll get right to the point. The video of you and Rennen Bradley has made quite an impression on Mr. Knight."

"Really?" *A good or bad impression?* she was tempted to ask.

"Really. It's not every day you see a petite woman take down an NFL player. I've watched it several times myself."

Ariana caught the admiring tone in Amanda's voice. "Oh." It didn't seem appropriate to say *thanks.*

"Mr. Knight would like to schedule a rematch between you and Rennen Bradley."

Her heart flipped as she gripped the phone. "What?"

"We'd like to do it up big with the press, the works."

Ariana shook her head back and forth. "I don't think so."

"Mr. Knight has given me the authorization to offer you a deal."

"I'm not interested."

"I think you might be interested in this, Ms. Sanchez," came Amanda's brisk reply. Before Ariana could respond, she continued.

"Mr. Knight will pay one hundred grand to you and one hundred grand to the charity of your choice."

Ariana gulped out a laugh. "Are you serious? He's willing to pay that much for me to spar with Rennen?" This was ludicrous! She clutched her neck. A hundred grand would go far in gym renovations and upgrades. She could hire another full-time instructor. And, it would be life-changing to some charities she could think of. She'd probably pick one that helped Down syndrome children because of Gracie.

"Is this agreeable to you, Ms. Sanchez?"

Ariana's head began to spin. Would Ace freak out if she did a rematch with Rennen? Probably no more than he was freaking out already that she'd fought him to start with. Of course, when Ariana and Rennen squared off on the practice field, she had no idea the match would be plastered all over the Internet. "When?"

"In two or three weeks. We'll do a big media campaign surrounding it."

It was already annoying to have the press lurking around. Ariana couldn't imagine what it would be like when they got wind of a rematch. Still, she could put up with a lot of things for a hundred grand. It was on the tip of her tongue to say *yes*. But then she remembered something Ace had said. *Never take the first offer.* If James Knight was willing to pay two hundred grand for a rematch off the cuff, he'd probably pay a lot more. Ariana could really use the money. It cost a lot to staff the classes and programs, leaving little for upgrades. A swanky new gym had opened a mere two miles from her gym a few months prior, hurting her enrollment. To stay at the top of her game, Ariana needed new equipment and maybe a lap pool. If she shot down the offer and demanded more, she ran the risk of losing this opportunity. She chewed on her inner cheek, trying to decide what to do.

"Tell him I'll do it for two hundred grand. That is, two hundred to me and two hundred to the charity of my choice."

"I'm not sure Mr. Knight will go for that. That's a lot of money."

Ariana grunted. "Yeah, it's a lot of money for you and me, but not for Mr. Knight."

"I'm only authorized to offer a hundred grand to each entity."

"I won't do it for a penny less than two hundred grand."

Long pause. "I'll have to talk to Mr. Knight and get back to you."

She'd probably just thrown away a hundred grand because of her stubbornness. But it wasn't in Ariana to retreat. *All in or nothing.* "You know where to find me. Goodbye," she said curtly, ending the call. When she handed it back to Beth, her hand was shaking.

"What was that about?"

Beth's mouth nearly dropped onto the floor when Ariana repeated the conversation. "He was gonna pay you a hundred grand to knock Rennen Bradley on his butt again, and you turned him down?"

Ariana rolled her eyes. "I know, crazy, right?" She waved a hand. "I'd knock him on his butt again for free," she joked. Secretly, she'd do it just so she'd have an excuse to see Rennen again, but she wasn't about to admit that.

Beth gave her an incredulous look. "I can't believe you turned that down. Do you know what amazing publicity that would be for the gym? I've had a dozen calls or more over the past couple days from women wanting to sign up for your self-defense class."

The corners of Ariana's lips turned down. "I hadn't thought about that." They were making plans to add another class to accommodate interest.

"Maybe you should call the lady back and accept the offer."

It only took a second for Ariana to make up her mind. "Nope, I don't think so. Rennen's a hot topic right now and James Knight's all about the publicity. You mark my word. He'll pay the two hundred grand."

Beth's eyebrows shot up, causing her forehead to wrinkle. "You mean four hundred grand? Two to you and two to charity?"

Ariana winced inwardly. Those were large amounts, even for James Knight. She'd probably made a huge mistake by not taking the offer right off. While she didn't relish the idea of putting on a circus performance for the media, the money would be awesome. And it was a simple match that would last all of five minutes. *Easy peasy*. Rennen had all but challenged her to a rematch on national television. A thrill shot down her spine as she thought of the prospect.

"Oh, my gosh!" Beth sat back in her seat, her eyes rounder than pancakes.

"What now?" Ariana grumbled. "Another reporter?"

"Not exactly."

Ariana's back was to the door. She turned to see what Beth was gawking at. Her own jaw went slack as he strolled in, a large smile on his face.

"Hey," Rennen began.

For an instant no words would come. Ariana just stood there, looking at him.

Rennen stepped up to the counter and glanced around. "Nice place."

Beth gave Ariana an odd look, which prompted her to action. "Thanks," she sputtered. Rennen was wearing athletic shorts and a fitted shirt that showed every ripple of his defined torso. Her gaze flickered over his rugged features, settling on the tantalizing scruff along his jaw. A few of the gym members in the weight area stopped working out and were staring in their direction. *Sheesh*. Rennen's presence was more distracting than the reporters.

Ariana drew her eyebrows together. "What're you doing here?"

"Joining your gym."

Her tongue seemed to cut off her windpipe as she gurgled. "What? You can't just waltz in here and join my gym!"

A trace of amusement lit his eyes, which looked more golden today than green. "Why not?" He leaned in, lowering his voice. "You're not discriminating against me because I'm white, are you?"

Beth sniggered, then put a hand over her mouth when she saw Ariana's blistering expression.

Ariana straightened her shoulders, glaring at Rennen. "Is this all some big joke to you?"

Rennen's smile vanished, but his lips quivered like he was trying not to laugh. "Absolutely not. I just want to get a workout."

She put her hands on her hips, assessing him. He had her over a barrel. Ariana had no choice but to let him join. She couldn't refuse service to anyone, no matter how much she wanted to. "This won't land you a date, if that's what you're thinking."

An indiscernible expression came over his features. "That's a little presumptive. I didn't mention anything about a date."

Heat flamed her face. He was really pushing her buttons. "Uh, huh. I know what you're doing. And it won't work."

He held up his hands. "I just wanna get a workout."

She turned to Beth whose eyes were shining with adoration as she looked at Rennen.

"Beth," Ariana barked.

Beth jumped, coming out of her daze. "Yes?"

"Can you get Rennen signed up?"

"You bet," she said quickly, a smile filling her face.

It was disgusting how the girls fell over Rennen. Even Beth was falling over him, and she wasn't easily impressed. *Why in the heck is Rennen so determined to pursue me?* Ariana wondered.

Tina, one of the instructors, rushed up to the front desk. She stopped in her tracks, a stupid grin curving her lips when she saw Rennen. "Hi."

He smiled. "Hi."

A dart of jealousy shot though Ariana. Tina was a fabulous instructor but loved to flirt with every guy who stepped foot in the gym. She'd be stuck to Rennen like glue.

Tina looked Rennen up and down with open admiration. "You look bigger in real life." She touched his arm. "Great biceps."

"Thanks," he said.

Ariana couldn't tell if he was pleased with Tina's compliment.

"So, what're you doing here?" Tina asked.

"I'm joining."

Tina's eyes lit up like she'd won the lottery. "That's fabulous," she gushed. She gave him a hopeful look. "You'll have to take one of my classes."

"Sure."

Ariana had all of this she could stand. Next, Tina would be prostrating herself at Rennen's feet, begging him to take her out on a date. She cleared her throat. "Tina, did you come up here for a reason?"

"Oh, yeah. Is Bart here? He normally helps me set up the bikes for my spin class."

"No, he's not coming in today." Ariana sighed, the weight of the situation settling on her. "I'll have to put up a sign saying Bart's class is cancelled. How many extra bikes do you have? Maybe a few of his people can join your class."

"Normally, I have four or five slots open," Tina said.

Not as many as Ariana hoped, but it would help. "Okay, we'll offer your class as an option. A few can join my class as well." Unfortunately, Ariana only had about three extra spaces. That left twenty or more people in Bart's class who'd have no place to go.

"What class does Bart teach?" Rennen asked.

Ariana was about to say that was none of his concern, but Tina spoke first. "Circuit training."

"I can teach the class," Rennen offered.

Ariana couldn't stop the brittle laugh from leaving her throat. "Seriously?"

"Seriously," Rennen said offhandedly, like it was no big deal.

There was no way Ariana was going to allow Rennen to teach a class. She pulled at her shirt. Things were getting way too complicated where he was concerned. If Ace got wind that Rennen was teaching at the gym, he'd go berserk. She felt like a big enough traitor as it was for having feelings for Rennen. She didn't want to keep adding insult to injury. Maybe it was a good thing she'd turned down Mr. Knight's offer. Just being around Rennen muddled her thinking. "Absolutely not. You're not certified."

"Come on," Tina urged, shooting Rennen an admiring look. "He's an NFL player. Circuit training is his life. How much more training does a person need?"

Rennen grinned. "She makes a good point."

"It would be good not to have to cancel Bart's class," Beth added timidly.

Ariana groaned. "Not you too."

She looked at Rennen. "Everything's crazy enough as it is with the press breathing down our necks. Do you really want to add this to it?"

The corners of his lips turned down. "Has the press been after you too?"

The concern in his eyes shot straight to her heart. He cared about her, a lot. She could see it in his face. Which is why she couldn't allow things to progress. She waved a hand. "Nothing I can't handle."

"It's been like a zoo here the past few days," Beth admitted.

Rennen pulled a face. "I'm sorry."

Ariana lifted her chin, attempting a smile. She wondered if he knew about the offer James Knight had made her. "Like I said, I've got it under control. I do," she snapped when she saw the silent exchange between Beth and Rennen.

Beth gave her a steely look. "You can get mad at me if you want, but I think you should let Rennen teach. The clients will love it. I mean, how often do people get to take a class from an NFL player? He's trying to do something nice for you. I think you should let him."

"Beth's right," Tina piped in, flashing Rennen a sultry smile like she could eat him in a single bite. She slipped her arm through Rennen's. "Come on, I'll show you the classroom."

"This is not a good idea," Ariana said, but her words fell on deaf ears as Tina led Rennen away. She spun around, her eyes blazing. "Why did you do that?"

Beth's face turned red. "I—I was only trying to help. You needed an instructor and he came in."

"I know what happened," she spat. She threaded her fingers through her hair, gripping her scalp. "This whole thing's getting out of control."

"Take it easy, it's one class."

She threw her hands in the air. "It's a lot more than that, I promise you."

"You like him."

She jerked. "What?"

Beth eyed her, not backing down. "You do. It's written all over your face."

"You're delusional," she countered, knowing Beth was right. She was pathetic ... weak. Her loyalty should be to Ace, at all costs. She glanced at the clock on the wall. "I've got to get ready for my class," she muttered. She'd spent too much time worrying about Rennen Bradley.

The phone rang and Beth answered. "Total Body Fitness. How may I help you?" Her eyes bulged. "Yes, she's right here." She put a hand over the receiver. "It's James Knight," she whispered.

The floor seemed to give way as Ariana fought to steady herself.

"Here." Beth handed her the phone.

She drew in a breath. "Ariana Sanchez," she said as professionally as she could.

"Hello, Ariana. This is James Knight." His voice was warm like they were old friends. "How've ya been?"

"Okay."

"I understand you spoke with my assistant Amanda."

"Yes."

"Good. Then the rematch is a go."

"What? No, I told her I'd do it if you paid me two hundred grand and my charity the same." She felt like a money grubber. But she wasn't going to be bulldozed into this without being well compensated.

He laughed. "Of course. The money's no problem."

She swallowed. "So, you're willing to pay my price?"

"Yes."

She gave Beth a thumbs up. Beth jumped up and down, squealing.

"Provided that you agree to one condition."

Her heart dropped. Ariana should've known this was too good to be true. She crossed her arms over her chest. "I'm listening," she said dryly.

"We want you to go on a date with Rennen."

She coughed, nearly choking on her own saliva. "W-what? Are you nuts?" Had the whole world gone crazy? "That's absurd."

He laughed. "Just kidding. Rennen asked me to say that to you when I called. He thought you'd get a kick out of it."

Her eyes narrowed. "Rennen knows about the rematch?"

"Of course. I spoke to him this morning ... err ... rather his PR firm. They think a rematch is a splendid idea, especially in light of Rennen's interview with Katie Moss."

Ariana drew her lips together in a tight line. It cut to think this was all a big PR stunt for him. Then again, she was doing it for the money. How could she fault Rennen for doing it for the publicity? On the upside, knowing this would keep things straight in her head, dispelling any illusions she had about Rennen's intentions.

"Good, it sounds like we're in agreement. You'll do the rematch," he confirmed.

"Yes. What about my payment?"

"Amanda will be in touch with you about the details. Typically, in these types of situations, we write you a check upon completion of the assignment."

Assignment. The word sounded so sterile. How many types of situations like this arose? Probably a lot. "Okay."

"Thanks. Have a nice day." He ended the call before she could respond.

"The rematch is on," Beth beamed, bringing her hands together.

"Yep, it looks that way."

7

Teaching a class was harder than he'd thought it would be. The trick was making sure not to push the students too hard but still making sure they got a good workout. Rennen glanced at the clock. Class ended on the hour, meaning he only had another seven minutes. *Thankfully*. He couldn't wait to get done with this so he could talk to Ariana. She was a hard nut to crack, but so darn sexy. He couldn't help but smile thinking about her feisty attitude. On the day of the Tiny Titans Football Camp he'd promised himself that he'd forget about her. Then when he realized she was at the camp, a surge of adrenaline spiked through him, all he could think about was getting out on the field with her. She was determined to shut him out of her life, at least that's what she kept saying. But her expressive eyes said otherwise. He could tell she liked him. It was crazy that he was so caught up in her. The all-consuming attraction made little sense, but he couldn't deny how he felt. Heck, he'd joined her gym and taught this class just so he could be next to her. Pathetic, he knew. But he couldn't seem to help himself.

He took the class through a series of stretching and breathing activities to cool them off. Finally, when the minute hand reached the blessed hour mark, he smiled. "And that's a wrap, folks. It was a pleasure being here today."

He was surprised when everyone clapped.

"That was fantastic," a peppy blonde said, a gigantic smile on her face. "My husband won't believe it when I tell him you taught the class."

"Will you be here next time?" a woman asked.

"I was just filling in for the instructor today."

A twinkle lit the woman's eyes. "Are you and Ariana an item?"

Briefly, he thought about saying *yes*, but Ariana would kill him. "No, just friends."

A few chuckles rippled through the room. "Sure you are," a woman in the back said with a wink.

Rennen just smiled. As the students filed out, he strode over to the bench along the wall and reached for the water bottle Tina had given him. He opened it and took a long swig. He set the bottle down, then placed his phone and car keys back in his pocket.

"How did it go?"

He jumped slightly as Ariana entered the room. Like him, she was sweaty from her workout. His eyes ran along the lines of her sculpted figure, slender shoulders, cut biceps, tapered waist, lean, muscular legs. "Pretty good, I think. The students seemed to enjoy it."

"I'll bet," she mumbled.

He cocked his head, a smile sliding over his lips. "What's that supposed to mean?" She was ready to fight him at every turn. He wondered how she'd react if he suddenly grabbed her and kissed her. No doubt she'd have him on the floor faster than he could draw a breath, but it would be worth it.

She frowned. "What's so funny?"

"You."

She cocked a sculpted eyebrow. "What do you mean?"

Rennen wondered how she could look so glamorous after a workout. She was wearing spandex shorts and a sleeveless shirt. Without her heels, she came to his chest. Her hair was wet where it touched her face. She tucked a strand of hair behind her ear, giving him a glimpse of her diamond stud earring. He shook his head. "You know, a simple *thanks* would suffice."

She perched a hand on her hip. "For what?"

"For teaching the class." He brought the water bottle to his lips and drained it. Then he crushed it in his hand.

Her dark eyes flashed. "You strong-armed me into that. But *thanks*," she said tartly.

"You're welcome." A beat stretched between them. "So, what's next on your schedule? Are you teaching more classes?"

"Yeah, I have another one at four."

"Anything after that?" He tried to sound casual.

"Nope, that's it for work."

His pulse throbbed like a bass drum against his neck. "I was thinking we might grab a bite to eat."

"No can do. Sorry, I have a date."

His heart lurched. "Really?"

"Really." She picked up a couple of empty water bottles on the bench, strode to the garbage can, and tossed them in. Rennen also tossed his bottle in the trash. Ariana picked up a towel someone had forgotten and slung it over her shoulder.

A date. He'd not anticipated that. A hot jealousy surged through him. "With who?"

She chuckled lightly. "That's none of your business."

She flipped off the lights and turned to leave. He rushed to keep up with her.

"Who's the date with?"

She made a face. "What does it matter?"

He caught hold of her arm, a feeling of desperation seizing him. "I'd like to know." He released her arm when she made a point of eyeing his hand with disapproval. He was coming on too strong, but couldn't seem to help himself.

She lifted her chin, defiance shining in her dark eyes. "Like I said, it's none of your business."

"Is it a first date? Or someone you know?" He felt like a schoolboy who'd just found out his girlfriend was going to the prom with someone else.

She quickened her pace down the hall, her body moving in stiff, jerky movements. "If you must know, it's with someone I met through Heart to Heart." She paused, throwing the towel into a box labeled "lost and found."

His brows shot up. "I thought you were done with that app, after the fiasco at the club."

She shrugged. "I thought I'd give it another try. After all, I signed a three-month contract. I'd might as well get my money's worth." She flashed a wicked grin. "This time, I made a point of stating no football players, so I should be good."

"Ouch," he muttered. Out of the corner of his eye, Rennen caught the interested glances from the people they passed. But he kept his focus on Ariana. He kept half expecting her to mention the rematch. Mr. Knight's assistant was supposed to call her today, but maybe she hadn't gotten through. When they reached the front, Ariana stepped behind the counter. He leaned against it, not ready to end the conversation.

She drummed her fingers against the wood. "Well, it's been good seeing you, Rennen, but I have work to do."

Their eyes met and for a fleeting moment, he got the distinct impression she wanted him to stay longer. *Fight for me*, she seemed to be saying. He placed a hand over hers. "Go out with me."

Something shifted in her eyes. He felt the longing pouring out of her into him. A rush of attraction buzzed through him. For one wild second, he thought she might say *yes*. But then Ariana's assistant stepped up, breaking the spell. Ariana quickly removed her hand, clearing her throat like she was embarrassed.

Rennen sighed. "Okay, you win. I'll leave you alone." A thrill shot through him when he saw the flicker of disappointment in her eyes. He smiled. "But I'll be back tomorrow and the day after that."

Her head shot up. "Don't you have something else better to do?" she snipped. "What about training?"

"Over by lunch every day. See ya tomorrow."

She gritted her teeth. "You're impossible."

His eyes caressed hers. "Yeah, I know."

When he reached the door, he glanced back over his shoulder. Ariana was watching him with an enigmatic expression. When she realized she'd been caught, she blinked a couple of times, quickly looking down at her paperwork.

As Rennen stepped out of the gym, a brilliant idea took shape. Something that would guarantee him a date with Ariana. Yes, it could work. What was the use of being a celebrity if he couldn't pull a few strings? He reached for his phone and called his PR rep at the DaVinci Agency. "Hey, Lainey, this is Rennen," he said when she answered. "I need you to work on something for me."

WITH EACH PASSING DAY, Ariana's willpower was weakening. She'd even taken to watching the clock, counting the hours until Rennen came to the gym. A couple of times, he'd taken her classes, which was unnerving. It was hard to concentrate on teaching when all she could think about was him, watching her with those magnetic eyes. The last thing she saw each night when she went to sleep was a flash of blonde curls and Rennen's devastating grin that melted her defenses. It was good she was dating other guys. That was the only way she'd be able to put Rennen out of her mind for good.

Rennen hadn't mentioned a word of their rematch. Mr. Knight's assistant called with a date for the match. It would take place two weeks from today. The time of day was yet to be determined. Reporters were still swarming the gym, especially since they'd learned that Rennen had joined. Ariana was worried her clients might be upset with all the attention, but they seemed to be okay with it, so long as they got to keep rubbing shoulders with Rennen. Enrollment had increased ten percent over the past week alone, and Ariana knew that was owed to having an NFL player there on a daily basis.

Ariana checked her reflection in the mirror, then picked up a makeup brush and gave her cheekbones a dusting of blush. Next, she applied lip-gloss, fluffed her hair, and put on a pair of gold, dangly earrings. Her past two dates with Heart to Heart had been okay, but nothing to write home about. Tonight, she was going out with a guy who had potential. She'd been texting back and forth for a couple of days with an attorney, Scott Jones, who seemed like a sharp guy. Ariana hinted that she'd like to see a photo of him, but he told her he wanted to keep her in suspense. It was good to have a distraction from Rennen. Scott seemed like a witty guy, and he enjoyed doing outdoor activities. They were meeting at a trendy Tex-Mex restaurant in Ft. Worth and were going to an indoor climbing wall afterwards. She figured any guy brave enough to go climbing on a first date must be in decent shape. She smoothed her hands down the red sundress and slipped on a pair of wedge sandals. Last, she reached for her perfume and pumped out a couple of squirts, stepping into the mist.

Scott offered to pick her up at her apartment, but she opted to meet him at the restaurant instead. She'd learned it was better to have her own car, in case she needed to make a quick get-away.

The restaurant was brimming with people when Ariana arrived. She'd only eaten at The Red Table once before, but remembered the food was good. If things went well with Scott, Ariana would have to take him to Los Tios to meet the family. Ace would be relieved to see that she'd moved past Rennen.

Ariana stepped up to the hostess. She was a little early. Scott wasn't due to arrive until seven and it was a quarter 'til.

"How many?"

"Two."

The hostess nodded. "Your name?"

"Sanchez."

The girl handed Ariana a buzzer. "It'll be about ten minutes."

"Okay, thanks."

She sat down in the waiting area, scoping out the restaurant. Scott told her he was blonde, tall, and would be wearing a blue, button-down shirt and jeans. His description sounded great. Ariana was a sucker for tall blondes. *Obviously*, her mind screamed as an image of Rennen rushed through her head.

Rennen had not come to the gym today, leaving a huge void ... and not just for Ariana. Beth, along with several of the instructors and clients, asked where he was. It was a little unnerving how quickly the staff at the gym, and many of the clients, had bonded with Rennen. Then again, he was a rising star. Maybe Rennen's absence today was owed to him finally getting the hint that she was off limits. Was he giving up? Her stomach tightened, disappointment shooting through her. She pushed the thoughts away, willing herself to focus on her upcoming date.

The buzzer went off. She stood and handed it to the hostess. *That was fast.* She'd only been waiting five minutes.

The hostess smiled, motioning to a girl standing beside her. "This is Nicole. She'll show you to your table."

"Thank you."

As soon as Ariana got seated, she sent Scott a text.

I got us a table.

He texted right back.

Awesome. Be there in five.

Flutters went through her stomach. She needed a win. Oh, how she hoped this would go well. A server in his early twenties approached the table. "Hello, my name's Mike. I'll be taking care of you tonight. Can I get you something to drink?" He pointed to the menu Ariana was holding. "We have a large selection of wines. And we have fountain drinks, raspberry lemonade, coffee, tea. Our beverages are listed on the back section of the menu."

"I'll have water with lemon."

He nodded. "Of course." Mike glanced at the empty seat across from her.

"My date will be here shortly," she said. "Would you bring him a water with lemon as well?"

"Certainly."

Ariana figured Scott could order something else if he wanted.

"Would you like to order an appetizer while you wait?"

"No thanks."

"I'll be right back with your drinks."

The ambiance of the restaurant was nice—trendy but not so modern that it felt cold. The lights were dim with soft music playing in the background. Ariana looked at the menu. Her stomach rumbled. She'd not eaten since lunch and was starving. The downside to teaching several classes each day was that she was a bottomless pit. She tried to remember what she'd gotten here before. The chicken enchiladas, maybe? The teriyaki salmon with wild rice looked good. Maybe add a side salad to go with it. Her mouth watered as she looked at the sweet potato chips with chipotle salsa. She remembered that from before because it was outstanding.

She glanced up to see Rennen striding toward her.

8

A riana's heart jumped into her mouth when Rennen sat down across from her.

A smile slid over his lips. "Hey." His eyes flickered over her. "You look fantastic. Red is definitely your color."

"You can't be here," she hissed, putting down the menu. "I have a date." Rennen was going to ruin everything.

He picked up the menu, his lips creasing into a quirky grin. "I know."

"Then you should know you can't be here. Scott will be here any minute."

Mike arrived with the drinks and placed them on the table. He looked at Rennen. "Would you like anything to drink besides water, sir?"

Rennen looked thoughtful. "What are the choices?"

As Mike ran through the list, Ariana's mind was a jumble. She couldn't believe Rennen had the audacity to follow her here. Scott would be here any minute. In fact, she was surprised he wasn't here already.

"I'll have raspberry lemonade."

"Would you like any appetizers?"

"No," Ariana blurted. "He's not staying."

Mike gave her a funny look.

Rennen smoothed out the awkwardness with a smile. "Yes, we'd love some of your sweet potato chips and the salsa that goes with it."

Mike jotted that down. "Excellent choice."

Rennen looked at Ariana. "They're fantastic. You'll love them."

She balled her fist, her fingernails digging into her palm.

"Are you ready to place your order, or do you need a few more minutes to look over the menu?" Mike asked.

"Give us a few more minutes," Rennen said.

Recognition lit Mike's eyes. "Hey, I know you. I saw you on the interview with Katie Moss. You're Rennen Bradley."

"Yes."

"It's a great honor to be your server," he gushed.

"Thank you." Rennen lowered his voice. "Hey, if you don't mind keeping that on the down low I'd appreciate it." He motioned at Ariana. "I'd like to have a nice evening with my lady."

"I'm not your lady," Ariana retorted.

"Sure, man. I'll keep it quiet," Mike said, his eyes gleaming like he'd seen his first Camaro. "Be back shortly with your drink and appetizer."

As Mike walked away, Ariana leaned forward. Her blood was pumping so fast it was making her dizzy. "What do you think you're doing? You can't just keep showing up and inserting yourself into my life. I have a date."

"I know." He took a long drink of water and placed the glass down with a plunk. "You're meeting Scott Jones, a patent attorney. And afterwards, you're going climbing."

Several things hit Ariana at once. First, he knew Scott's name, profession, and their agenda. Second, it registered that he was wearing a blue, button-down shirt. An incredulous laugh bubbled in her throat. "You're Scott Jones."

Rennen sat back in his seat, a sheepish grin on his handsome face. "I hope you're not too disappointed."

"H-how," she sputtered. She thought back to the texts she and

Scott—Rennen had been exchanging for the past few days. Witty ... charming ... easy to connect with. She should've known. She went hotter than a penny on the asphalt in July. "How could you?" she seethed. She couldn't believe Rennen had gone to the trouble to pretend he was someone else. How he even managed it was beyond her. That was it! No more Heart to Heart! She was demanding a full refund.

"You left me little choice."

She arched an eyebrow. "There's always a choice. I should've known Scott was too good to be true," she muttered, reaching for her purse. She moved to stand, but Rennen caught her arm. A jolt pinged through her when their skin touched.

"Don't leave. Please."

She eyed him. "Give me one good reason to stay."

"Because it's my birthday. And I don't want to be alone."

She saw the vulnerability in his eyes, knew somehow in a way that defied words that he was telling the truth. A lump of emotion formed in her throat. Birthdays were a big deal in her family. The year before, her parents had thrown her a huge party at Los Tios. She sat back down, knowing there was no way she could let him spend tonight alone.

"I'm sorry I tricked you."

His hand was still over hers. This thing with them ... she didn't know what to do about it. The more she tried to escape from Rennen, the stronger their connection grew. Despite her best effort to hold it back, a rush of excitement thrummed through her veins. She felt alive and a little reckless, much like she'd felt on the first night they met.

His lips curved in an easy smile. "I just wanna have dinner, get to know you more. Is that too much to ask?" His eyes pled with hers. "I mean, we're here. We might as well eat."

She cocked an eyebrow. "And afterwards?"

"We'll go climbing, just like we planned."

She pursed her lips. "Do you even like climbing, or were you just throwing that out there because you knew I'd bite?"

"No, I truly enjoy climbing."

She removed her hand from his, giving him a steely look. "So, Scott ... what would you like for dinner?"

His eyes seemed to collect the light from the fixtures above as he grinned. "My middle name is Scott."

She cocked her head, not ready to let him off the hook. "And your last name?"

He waved a hand, and she caught a trace of something—annoyance or perhaps sadness—in his eyes. "Bradley was a name I was given by some social worker. My last name's a placeholder. It might as well be Jones."

"What about your first name? Was that given to you by a social worker also?"

"Yeah, I suppose so. It had to have been, right?"

Ariana couldn't imagine what he'd been through. She felt a wave of sympathy, but tried hard not to show it. She had a feeling that Rennen wouldn't tolerate anyone feeling sorry for him. And she didn't blame him. "How about the attorney part?"

"Well, before football took center stage, I was planning on studying law."

"I see. Anything else I should know about you?" she quipped.

His eyes locked with hers. "Once I set my sights on something, I never let it go."

The promise in his voice sent a surge of adrenaline through her. Heat fanned her face, and with that heat came a longing she could scarcely contain. In that moment, she got the crazy feeling that everything she'd been looking for was sitting right in front of her, a hair's breadth away. All she had to do was let herself go and embrace it.

Mike returned with Rennen's raspberry lemonade and the appetizer, breaking the spell. Ariana sighed inwardly. She'd almost lost it there. Rennen was really throwing her for a loop. She'd have to do a better job of keeping her guard up. Mike took their dinner orders. Ariana chose the salmon and Rennen fish tacos.

"You're gonna love these sweet potato chips," Rennen said, dipping one in the salsa and placing it in his mouth.

"Yes, I do."

He looked surprised. "You've had them before?"

"Yep. I've been here once before."

"With another guy?"

"Yes." She'd come here with Paul, her ex-boyfriend.

The corners of Rennen's mouth turned down. "That's too bad."

"Why's that?" She dipped a chip in salsa and plopped it in her mouth, savoring the combination of sweet and salty with the complex tanginess of the chipotle. *Delicious.*

"I was hoping to take you somewhere you've never been before ... especially with someone else."

He looked adorable when he was pouting. She gave him a reassuring smile. "It's still great." She could've added that she'd never felt so excited to be on a date before. Everything was enhanced. The very air held a crackle of anticipation, the food tasted better, every sensation was heightened. *Down, girl*, she warned herself. *Geez. How many of these little talks do I need to have with myself before it sinks in?* She looked at Rennen, surprised he was studying her. "What?"

"You're so beautiful."

The statement was spoken soft and husky, warming her through to her bones. "Thanks," she murmured, her eyelashes sweeping over her cheekbones. She reached for her water and took a sip, trying to break the intense connection between them. A couple of minutes later, she realized a silver-haired man with a beard sitting at the table across the room was staring at them. When she gave him a pointed look, he turned his attention to his menu. She scowled.

"What?"

"There's a man spying on us." Truthfully, if felt good to have something other than Rennen on which to focus. She'd have to keep applying that tactic.

Rennen sighed. "Probably a reporter." He turned to look.

"The one with the menu in front of his face," Ariana said. "He's hiding behind it now that he knows I caught him." She homed in on the man with laser-like focus.

Rennen laughed.

She turned her attention back to Rennen, giving him a questioning look.

"You're like a little guard dog."

She started blinking, her shoulders tensing. "Is that a compliment or insult?"

"A compliment to the highest degree. I admire you for it." His eyes held hers. "Truly." A wry grin tugged at his lips. "It's kind of ironic, the very thing I admire you for—your fierce loyalty to your brother—is the very thing keeping you from me."

The words were spoken so softly Ariana couldn't be sure she'd heard him correctly. She lifted her chin, eyeing him. "I could never betray my brother."

He brought his lips together in a tight line. "I know that." He peered into her eyes. "I would never ask you to."

Her heart began to pound. "Just being here with you is a betrayal of sorts."

"I don't see it that way at all. And I can't imagine that Ace sees it that way either. Every single player on the team is replaceable at the drop of the hat. Our necks are on the chopping block 24/7. The best we can hope for is to ride the wave as long as we can. Ace had a much longer ride than most. He should be celebrating the victory."

She tensed, surprised at how quickly the anger surfaced. "Don't presume to tell me what Ace should be feeling."

He held up his hands. "Okay." She was surprised when a stupid grin washed over his face.

"What?"

"How do you do that?"

Her eyebrow shot up. "What?"

"Get fired up so fast." He chuckled. "I wish I could bottle up your torque and use it on the field."

A laugh burst from her throat, releasing the tension. "You're crazy." So he liked her torque. That was flattering ... sort of. Her thoughts went back to the silver-haired man as she shot a glare in his direction. "Doesn't it drive you crazy that reporters are always following you?" Her brows shot down in a V. "They're like vultures."

"It's been bad the past few days," he admitted. "Ever since the interview with Katie Moss. Before that, it was rare that people outside the sports world recognized me. But now ..."

"You're becoming a household name," she finished for him. There was something she'd wanted to ask Rennen since watching the interview. Even as she wondered if she should mention it, the words spilled out. "What you said about your nickname 'the Ghost.' That really got me." Her voice quivered slightly. "To be perfectly honest, I was kind of surprised you talked about something that personal on TV."

He nodded, his features tightening. "I hadn't planned on mentioning it, but it just came out." His lips thinned. "When I watched the recording, I regretted saying it. But what can you do, right?" He let out a self-deprecating chuckle. "I guess that's why Katie is so popular. She puts people at ease to the point where they spill their guts."

Without thinking, Ariana touched his hand. "I'm really sorry about all that you've gone through."

His jaw worked, and she could tell he was trying to put a cap on his emotions. "Thanks. It's life, I suppose." A sardonic smile twisted over his lips. "I guess that's why they call life a four-letter word, huh?"

She chuckled. "Evidently." The conversation lagged, each of them lost in their own thoughts. There was something about the interview that had been bothering Ariana. She had no right to bring it up, but felt compelled to. "Are you sure you don't want to find out who your parents are?" She knew she'd tread on forbidden territory the moment the words left her mouth. His eyes went flat like they had during the interview, and she could tell he was withdrawing. That was his coping mechanism. He removed his hand from hers.

"Very sure," he countered. "I have no use for a mother who abandoned her baby. Leaving me to fend for myself."

The bitter hurt in his voice stabbed through her heart. The words rushed out. "I just think you owe it to yourself to find out where you came from. So you can begin to heal." She couldn't stand the thought of him going through life, feeling like a ghost—not knowing who he really was.

Mike arrived with the food. Silence overtook them as they commenced eating. The food was excellent, but Ariana couldn't enjoy it. Finally, she couldn't tolerate Rennen's stoniness any longer. "I'm sorry. I didn't mean to butt into your business."

The air seemed to hold its breath as they looked at each other. Finally, his features softened. "It's okay." A slight smile touched his lips. "It's hard to talk about."

"I'm sure." She was tempted to press him more about finding out about his parents but knew it would only tick him off. Besides, she didn't have the right to question him about his past. They weren't a couple.

Thankfully, the conversation drifted to lighter topics. Ariana found herself talking about her boisterous family and their restaurant. How her mother was always barking orders to everybody but had a heart of gold. How her dad was quiet and reserved. Rennen talked about growing up in Austin. It was obvious he was super fond of the Boyd family who'd practically adopted him.

When the meal was over a contented buzz settled over Ariana as she leaned back in her seat. "That was excellent. Great choice."

"Thanks. It was great."

She clutched her stomach. "I'll have to let this food settle before we go climbing."

"Amen." Rennen leaned forward. "There's something I'd like to ask you." His voice choked a little like he had a frog in it. He cleared it and began again. "This weekend is Gary's sixtieth birthday."

Gary Boyd was the father of Rennen's best friend in high school— and probably the closest thing Rennen had to a father.

He searched her face. "I'd like for you to go with me."

She drew in a ragged breath, hardly believing that he'd ask her that. An incredulous laugh escaped her lips. "We're on our first date ... sort of. But only because I didn't realize I was going out with you." She gave him a sharp look. "And now you're asking me to go away with you for the weekend?" Her voice escalated as she shook her head. *Really.* This was too much.

A tiny smile crept over his lips. "I guess no one can accuse me of having alligator arms, huh?"

She tipped her head. "I've never heard that before."

"It's a term used when a pass receiver's too chicken to extend his arms all the way to make a catch, mostly because he's anticipating a hit by a defensive player."

"The *all in or nothing* approach." She thought of what he'd said earlier about setting his sights on something and never letting it ago. A part of her found that thrilling and a little scary.

His smile broadened. "Exactly."

She couldn't help but feel a grudging admiration for Rennen's analogy; she'd used the same strategy in her negotiations with Mr. Knight. The tactic had certainly worked in Ariana's favor there. Too bad it wouldn't work for Rennen. Under another circumstance, she'd jump at the chance to go, but as it was ... She tried to think of a way to let him down easily. "Even if I wanted to go, I couldn't get off work."

"I've got it all worked out with Beth. She can arrange for someone to fill in for your classes, and she can hold down the fort. It would just be for three days—Friday through Sunday."

"Ah, so you and Beth have been conspiring behind my back." She drew her lips together. "Hmm ... I'll have to talk to her about that."

"No, don't do that. Beth's only trying to help."

She sighed. "I know." Beth was amazing. Ariana was so blessed to have her. Like Rennen said, she was acting in what she thought was Ariana's best interest. She just didn't understand the full scope of the situation. Rennen would have to get used to disappointment because there was no way they could ever be together.

"I just don't think I can afford to take off."

"Come on," he urged. "You know you wanna go." He gave her a crooked grin. "And after our rematch, you'll be rolling in the dough."

"I was wondering when you were gonna bring that up." She thought of the feeling of elation that had swelled through her when Mr. Knight's assistant told her about the rematch and then how that elation had turned to acid in Ariana's mouth when she realized she was a PR stunt.

His watchful eyes assessed her. "What's wrong? I thought you'd be all too happy to kick my butt on national TV."

"Oh, I am. Believe me." She forced a smile. "Anything for publicity, right?" She had no right to judge him. Hadn't she thought about how the publicity would be good for the gym? And she certainly needed the money. Her feelings on the subject made no sense. And yet, she couldn't seem to stop herself from having them. She was pathetic.

Amusement lit his eyes. "Is that what you think this is? A way to gain publicity?"

Her gaze met his. "Isn't it?"

He touched his napkin, fingering it absently. "I mean, the publicity can't hurt either of us, right? And don't forget that a substantial amount of money is going to charity."

She concentrated on the napkin under his fingers. "Right." She got the feeling he could see right through her. Knew how hypocritical she was being.

A teasing light came into his eyes. "There are other perks."

"Such as?"

"The more full-body contact the two of us have, the better."

Heat crawled up her neck. "You're such a pig." She couldn't stop a smile from curving her lips.

He shrugged. "Just saying."

She leaned forward, the thrill of the match seeping into her pores. "I'm gonna enjoy laying you out on national TV."

He also leaned forward, his eyes dancing. "You talk big for a little girl."

"Uh, huh," she drawled.

"I'm comfortable enough with my masculinity to handle whatever comes." He cocked his head like he'd just thought of something. "I should sign up for one of your classes, so you can give me some pointers."

A laugh rumbled in her throat. "Pointers on how to beat me? I don't think so."

A grin filled his face. "In all seriousness, I'm glad you agreed to the rematch. And I'm glad you socked it to James, made the old man fork over more money."

She kept a straight face. "Yeah, I kind of felt bad for charging him anything. After all, I would've kicked your butt for free."

He burst out laughing. "I know you would have."

Laughter rumbled in her throat. It felt good to release some of the tension. She was glad the rematch was out in the open. Of course, there was still Ace to deal with. She'd been avoiding him because she wasn't sure how he'd feel about it. But she'd have to talk to him soon.

Rennen studied her. "So, will you go with me to Austin?"

She sighed. *Not this, again.* She shook her head, ready to turn him down, but he held up a hand.

"You don't have to give me an answer tonight. Just think about it." A grin tugged at his lips. "After all, if you're gonna turn me down, I'd rather it not be on my birthday."

Relief splattered over her. She wouldn't have to tell him *no* tonight. They could hold onto the illusion a little longer. She allowed herself a second to rove over his face, memorizing his features— heavyset brows, thin nose that had a bump like it had been broken before, strong jaw. His mane of untamed curls. Her eyes trailed down his masculine neckline to his prominent Adam's apple. Her throat went dry as she swallowed. She was so conflicted right now, she didn't know which way was up. "Happy birthday." It went through her mind that Rennen couldn't know the real date of his birthday. Someone had probably assigned him a date. It was remarkable that he'd accomplished all he had, despite his upbringing. He was really some-thing—one in a million.

His eyes sparkled in a challenge as he placed a hand over hers. "You ready for our next activity?"

She met his gaze full on. "Does a cat have a climbing gear?" She linked her fingers through his. Not the smartest move, but she couldn't seem to help herself. She was growing weary of constantly battling this attraction.

He chuckled. "Yes, I suppose it does." Pleasure lit his eyes as he tightened his grip on her hand. Then he looked around. "Now where is that server with our check?"

She cocked an eyebrow. "What? Skipping out before dessert?" Her lips formed a mock pout. "And I was looking forward to the birthday song."

"No, thanks." He shuddered. "I think we'll skip that part."

She wrinkled her nose. "I'll let you off ... this time. But only because you're taking me climbing."

9

Rennen kept his eyes fixed on Ariana who was climbing like a cat up the wall. When they arrived at the climbing wall, he and Ariana changed into athletic clothes. Ariana had her own climbing shoes, but Rennen rented a pair. Rennen tightened his grip on the rope as he pulled down. Ariana climbed so quickly that it was a challenge to keep the slack out of the rope as he belayed her. Rennen wasn't an expert at climbing but he'd done it enough to know that the key to belaying was to make sure the rope stayed taut, so the harness would catch the climber in the event of a fall. Of course, with Ariana that was unlikely. She could've climbed without the harness and been just fine.

Rennen marveled that someone so petite could be so tough and feisty. Ariana had been shocked and outraged when she realized her date was with him. And yet, he'd caught the longing in her eyes when he invited her to go with him to Austin. Ariana was definitely battling some demons where he and Ace were concerned. Rennen liked Ace and hadn't set out to do him harm. When Rennen was traded to the Titans, he felt honored to play second string to such a great player, never dreaming that he'd get the opportunity to take Ace's place.

From what Rennen could tell, Ace seemed level-headed—a realist who understood the nature of the game. Sure it was awkward for Rennen and Ariana to be together, considering the circumstance, but life rarely worked out neatly. It was hard and messy and you just had to keep fighting your way through it to get to the top. And then when you reached the top, it still wasn't over. Because then you had to fight tooth and nail to stay there.

Everything Rennen had told Ariana earlier about the NFL was true. His neck was on the chopping block and the axe would fall if he couldn't perform. Monroe, his agent, had fought for as much up-front money as they could get. But like many contracts with unknown players, Rennen's two-year contract was predominantly performance based. Which is why he needed to remain focused on his training rather than getting too caught up in his feelings for Ariana. He sighed. Who was he kidding? Ariana was all he could think about. He'd not planned on inviting her to Austin, mostly because he knew he didn't have a prayer of her going. Still, the words had come out. And now, he was hopeful that she might actually go. He would love to show her off to the Boyds, get Warren's take on her. Ariana was warming up to Rennen, slowly but surely. He'd nearly wet his pants when she linked her fingers through his at the restaurant, but he acted like it was no big deal because he didn't want to scare her away.

Rennen wondered if he should pay Ace a visit. Once Ace realized how much Rennen cared about his sister, he was sure to come around. It was crazy how hard and fast Rennen had fallen for Ariana. Aside from her stunning beauty and feisty nature, she was a good person ... loyal to those she loved. And loyalty was everything to Rennen. Plus, she wasn't some cleat chaser after Rennen for his status or money. Rennen had lost count of the number of girls that had only been after him because he was an NFL Player. He couldn't help but chuckle at the irony. His football status was what was keeping Ariana from him.

Ariana reached the top and rappelled down. Rennen glanced over and noticed two twenty-something girls giving him the eye from across the room. When they realized he'd noticed them, they smiled and waved. He could tell from the looks on their faces that they recognized him. *Sheesh.* He wasn't used to all the attention. It was getting old ... fast! He gave them a courtesy nod, then turned back to Ariana.

Her dark eyes sparked mischief as she laughed, casting a glance toward the girls. "The minute I leave your side, you get a collection of women falling at your feet." Casually, she touched his arm, the warmth from her fingertips seeping into his skin.

He leaned in, wiggling his eyebrows. "Then maybe you should never leave my side."

An impish grin tugged at her lips. "Maybe."

Was she saying what he thought she was? A thrill shot through him as his eyes held hers. "That was some climbing. Is there anything you can't do?"

She wrinkled her nose. "Well, according to my mom, I'm not the greatest at making tamales or tortillas."

He laughed. "I suppose it wouldn't be fair for one woman to have all of the talents."

She shook her head. "You're quite the charmer, Goldie Locks." She touched one of his curls, then blinked like she'd realized what she'd done. Her hand dropped down by her side as she looked up the length of the wall. "Your turn."

He grimaced. "After your flawless climb?" He shook his head. "I'm afraid I may never hear the end of the teasing after you see how bad I am at climbing."

"It's okay. I'll give you a free pass since it's your birthday. I won't be too critical of you."

He laughed. "Too critical, huh?"

She winked. "Yeah." She motioned with her head. "Go for it, big guy. Vamanos."

"I hear ya." He dipped his hands in chalk and rubbed them together. His pulse drummed against his neck, and he felt like he did right before the kick-off at the beginning of a game. He looked up the wall. The top seemed impossibly far away. He reached for the knobs at his eye level and used his arms to heave himself up.

"Remember," Ariana said, "you don't pull with your hands, but push with your feet."

"Oh, yeah. Thanks," he mumbled offhandedly. He'd forgotten that little tidbit of information. But Ariana was right. It was much easier to push with his legs. And as it happened, his legs were used to carrying the brunt of the work. Once Rennen got past the first few handholds, he got in a good rhythm. He was pleasantly surprised at how easy it was to ascend the wall. He'd not climbed since high school, but it was like riding a bike. It all came flooding back. He reached the top in record time. When he rappelled back down and his feet touched the ground, he felt a burst of pride when he saw the look of admiration in Ariana's eyes.

"Bad at climbing, huh?" she mused. She clucked her tongue. "Tell me, Rennen Bradley. Is there anything you can't do?"

He loved the playful glint in her eyes. "Tamales and tortillas. I'm terrible at making those." He stepped out of the harness and handed it to the teenage boy, manning the wall. "Thanks."

The guy nodded, turning his attention to the next person in line.

Ariana's eyes rounded as she laughed. "You're terrible." She gave him a playful shove.

"Hey now," he growled. He tried to grab her arm, but she darted out of his reach. "You're quick." He chuckled. "But not quick enough." He caught her, encircling her waist with his arm. A broad smile split his lips. "I've got you now," he murmured, looking into her eyes.

She laughed. "Yes, you do. What now?"

He began to sway. "Well, we could dance."

She wrinkled her nose. "Here, in the middle of the climbing gym?"

"Why not?"

She threw back her head, adventure twinkling in her deep chocolate eyes. "Yeah, why not."

He leaned down. "Or I could just kiss you."

Her eyes widened, and he feared he'd pushed her too far. But then she smiled. "Why don't you?"

He jerked slightly, happiness tumbling through him. He didn't have to be asked twice. He leaned in and gave her a slow, searching kiss. A tender ache swept over him as he drank her in. He got the feeling that he could never get enough of her. She responded by slipping her arms around his neck and threading her fingers through his hair. When they pulled away, Ariana glanced around, her cheeks flaming.

"I'm sure we're causing quite a spectacle," she said with a half-laugh.

"Yeah, I guess so." Rennen didn't care. All he cared about was the woman standing in front of him—part warrior, part fairy. Tender, yet tough. All he knew in this moment was that Ariana Sanchez was consuming every last inch of him. "Go with me to Austin," he implored.

"Okay."

He swallowed. Had he heard her correctly? He searched her face, saw her hesitation, felt her longing. "You will?"

The hesitation gave way to certainty as she smiled, sending a beam of sunlight shooting into his heart. "Yes."

A feeling of exultation sang through to his toes and he felt like he could fly. He didn't try to hide the Texas-sized grin that spilled over his lips. "I'm crazy about you, Ariana," he said softly.

"I'm crazy about you too," she admitted.

He let out a whoop and picked her up, spinning her around.

A rich and lusty unbridled laugh sounded in her throat, sending his heart soaring.

"You're gonna love Austin. And the other surprise I have in store for you."

Interest lit her eyes, making her look like a young girl. "Surprise? What kind of surprise?"

He pumped his eyebrows. "Oh, no. I can't tell you that. You'll have to wait and see."

She chuckled. "All right." She studied his face. "Dinner ... climbing ... what's next, birthday boy?"

He grinned. "I thought we'd take Red for a spin, let her stretch her legs a little. Whaddaya say? You game?"

Her eyes danced. "My mama warned me about guys like you. Fast cars ... fast guys." She clucked her tongue. "Hmm ... what's a girl to do?" She cocked her head. "I'll go under one condition."

"Oh, yeah? What's that?"

A smile broke over her face. "I get to drive."

"I think we can arrange that," he laughed.

ARIANA THREW BACK the covers and dragged herself out of bed. She needed a very large and very strong cup of coffee. She padded to the kitchen, stifling a yawn. After she and Rennen took his car for a spin, they went dancing at the karaoke club until two in the morning. She'd fallen asleep the minute her head hit the pillow, drifting off to a blissful slumber, secure in the knowledge that she and Rennen would find a way to be together. In the cold light of day, however, things weren't so clear.

A trickle of anxiety ran down her spine, but she pushed it away. Her mind ran back through the events of the night before. One minute, she and Rennen were joking around. He was trying to catch her and she darted out of his reach. The next minute, his arms were around her, and they were kissing. She'd lost all reason at that point, promising him she'd go to Austin. Her hand went to her mouth. She could still feel the burn from Rennen's lips. No doubt she was crazy about him. Maybe even loved him, a little. Last night was magical.

When the coffee was done, she poured herself a cup and took a long sip. She'd have to find a way to break the news to Ace. Surely he'd understand. Ace was so madly in love with Silver he couldn't see straight. He'd pursued Silver despite all the obstacles that were against them. He'd understand that she felt the same way about

Rennen ... wouldn't he? She needed to talk to Ace today, before things got too far out of control.

She wrapped her fingers around the coffee mug appreciating the warmth, as she sat down at the table. She heard her phone ringing from her bedroom. Oh, well. She'd let it go to voicemail. It was good to just sit here and relax. She tucked a leg underneath her as she lifted the mug to her lips and took another drink. How in the heck was she going to explain this to Ace? Her phone rang again. She ignored it, running the hypothetical conversation through her mind. Like Rennen said, Ace knew the stakes ... knew that his time in the NFL would eventually come to an end. If Rennen hadn't taken his place, someone else would have.

She let out a deflated breath. Even in her own ears, her defense came out flat. She felt like such a traitor. Could she really follow her heart at the expense of her brother? It was so unfair to be put in his situation. In fact, it made her fighting mad. She scowled, taking another swig of coffee. She'd tried to resist Rennen—put up a good fight. But she couldn't deny her feelings for him. No one had ever made her feel this way before. At first, she'd chalked the whole thing up to an intense attraction. But that was only the tip of the iceberg. Her phone rang again. The caller wasn't giving up. She hurried to her bedroom and grabbed the phone from her dresser. It was her mother.

"Hello?" she answered the instant before the call dropped.

"Ariana, where've you been? I've been calling all morning."

Ariana's head throbbed dully across the bridge of her nose. "I slept in." She sat down on the edge of the bed, running a hand through her hair. She needed to shower and get ready. Thankfully, she didn't have to teach any classes today, but she still needed to stop by the gym to check on everything. Poor Rennen had training this morning. She could only imagine how tired he must be. She smiled thinking of how he'd pouted a little when he told her how early he'd have to get up this morning. She'd rubbed it in, saying that she could sleep in.

"You and that NFL player are all over the news."

Ariana's heart jumped in her throat. "What?"

Her mom's mouth started going a mile a minute. "Que pasa with you and that chico? How could you do this to Ace? Increíble! I never thought I'd see the day when my own hija would throw her hermano under the bus. Aye, yai, yai." She let out several long strings of English and Spanish curses mixed together.

Ariana stumbled to her feet, her mind spinning. "Where's the article?" she barked. She grabbed her laptop and slumped back down on the bed.

"The Dallas Star."

She opened the computer, her fingers flying over the keyboard as she went to the newspaper website. Her heart sank. There it was, the first article. A picture of her and Rennen, lips locked at the climbing gym. Tears stung her eyes as she read the headline, *The Ghost Takes It All.* She skimmed through the article, a venomous fire simmering in her veins.

"Rennen Bradley, A.K.A. the Ghost didn't stop at taking Ace Sanchez's spot on team, he's going for his sister as well. What's next? Ace's palatial home in The Reserve?"

"W-hat?" she spat. "The Reserve? Really?" Hot prickles covered Ariana and she had the surreal feeling of being separate from her body, watching the scene unfold from a distance.

There were several pictures of her and Rennen. Photos of them getting in Rennen's car. Photos at the karaoke club. The end of the article talked about their upcoming rematch, with the reporter speculating that the whole thing was a big publicity stunt cooked up by James Knight to take attention away from his daughter and team trainer Hailey Knight and her marriage to Brady Giles, new Titan cornerback who transferred from New England.

Ariana realized her mother was speaking. "Why did you go out with him?" Her voice escalated. "Kiss him? I thought you were gonna stay away from him."

The accusations cut holes in Ariana's heart as a wave of nausea pummeled over her. She'd been so stupid and naïve to think she and Rennen could somehow work this out. "Mom," she croaked. "I've gotta let you go."

Fabiana belted out a few more paragraphs, but Ariana couldn't process a word of it.

"I'll talk to you later," she said, ending the call in the middle of Fabiana's sentence.

Ariana sat on the bed, looking straight ahead. A curious numbness settled over her and then came the waterfall of hurt. Her face caved as she gave way to the sobs rising in her chest. She curled up on her bed and let the grief overtake her.

10

The bewitching hour was almost here. Ariana glanced at the clock on the wall. It was twenty-five minutes to three. Had everything not fallen apart, she'd be on her way to the gym right now to meet Rennen to go to Austin. She scowled, pushing back the wall of tears behind her eyes. She glanced at the movie playing on the TV, not seeing a thing. She reached in the bag beside her and grabbed a handful of barbecue potato chips, shoving them in her mouth.

For the past couple of hours, she'd sat here on the couch, munching on junk food, hoping it would dull the pain in her heart. So far, it wasn't working. She glanced at the wadded candy bar wrappers and empty carton of mint, chocolate-chip ice cream. All she'd managed to do was give herself a major stomach ache. She felt like a beached whale. Ariana swallowed the chips with a swig of Dr. Pepper, straight from the two-liter bottle. *All in or nothing.* A tear escaped the corner of her eye as she swiped it away. She'd tried the all-in approach and it had gotten her a big, fat nothing.

Ever since the blasted story broke about Ariana and Rennen on the night of his birthday, she'd avoided him. They'd talked once on the phone. He told her that while things looked bad, it would blow over as soon as the press got wind of another story to chase instead. He'd said he was coming over that instant to check on her, but she asked him to give her a few days to sort things out in her mind. She knew if she told Rennen straight out that they were through, he'd pursue her relentlessly. But this way, she could stall him until she built enough resolve to really let him go. She'd still not talked to Ace, but Fabiana said plenty on behalf of the entire family. Ariana felt like a complete louse for betraying Ace, but she was also betraying herself and Rennen too. There was just no winning in this situation.

Rennen sent her a text earlier this morning, saying that he really wanted her to go with him to Austin. When she didn't respond, he sent another message.

I'll be at the parking lot of your gym from 2:30 to 3:00. If you don't come, then I'll know that's your answer.

Thinking of him sitting there, waiting for her, tore her up inside. She reached for another handful of chips. Her phone rang. Her heart jumped, thinking it was Rennen, but it was Paul. She sighed heavily, clicking the button on the side to silence the ringer. This was the second time in two days Paul had called. The first time, he left her a message telling her he missed her and wanted to catch up. No doubt the news about her and Rennen was causing him to have regrets about the one who got away. After spending time with Rennen, Ariana couldn't imagine going out with Paul or any other guy. Now that she'd experienced what it was like to walk in bright sunlight she couldn't go back to life in the clouds.

"Hey, I hope you don't mind that I let myself in."

She jumped, looking up at Ace. "Hey." She ran a hand through her hair and tugged at her shirt as she sat up straight and removed her feet from the coffee table. She could only imagine how pathetic she looked right now, still wearing pajamas with the evidence of her carb binge scattered around her.

Ace plopped down in a nearby chair, his dark eyes flickering over her. "You look like crap."

A humorless laugh escaped. "I feel like crap." She took another swig of Dr. Pepper.

Ace motioned at the two-liter bottle in her hand, two-thirds empty. "It's a good thing you don't drink alcohol, or we might have a problem."

Her eyes narrowed. "Whatever," she mumbled. She leaned forward and placed the bottle on the coffee table.

He brought his hands together. "So, what's new with you?"

She laughed. "Seriously?" She shot him a dark look. "Don't try to act like you don't know exactly what's going on. And before you say anything, I'm sorry." Her voice caught. "I didn't set out to betray you." She swallowed the lump in her throat, but unfortunately, couldn't hold back the treacherous tears that rolled down her cheeks. Hastily, she wiped them away with the palms of her hands. "I know you think I'm horrible because I went out with Rennen, even after I knew who he was."

Ace studied her with an enigmatic expression. "You really care about him, don't you?"

A harsh chuckle escaped her lips. "Is it that obvious? Yeah," she admitted, "I do." She forced a smile. "Of all the guys in Dallas/Ft. Worth, I have to fall for the one who's off-limits." She let out a long breath, trying to stay the quiver in her voice. "But you don't have to worry. It's really over this time."

He rubbed a hand across his jaw, looking thoughtful. "Yeah, I was afraid you'd say that."

"Oh, I mean it," she countered. "Truly. You can tell Mom too." Her brows scrunched. "I'm sick of her harassing me about it." She placed the bag of chips on the floor, then drew her legs to her chest, wrapping her arms around her knees. She looked at the TV, pretending to take interest in the movie playing. But she could feel Ace watching her.

She spun around, glaring at him. "What?"

"Are you really gonna sit there feeling sorry for yourself all day?"

She lifted her chin, eyeing him. "Well, if I am, it's none of your business."

He just kept staring at her.

"What?" she barked.

A smile tugged at his lips. "Go after him, you dummy!"

She flinched, not sure she'd heard him correctly. "What did you say?"

His lips gave way to a large smile. "You heard me. Do I need to get a pitcher of ice water and dump it over your head, the way you did to me when you told me to go after Silver?"

Her mind whirled like an out-of-control merry-go-round. "You're telling me I need to go after Rennen?" Maybe the carb overload had fried her brain and she was in some wish-fulfillment stage of a dream.

"That's exactly what I'm saying. That is, if you care about him as much as I think you do."

Hope thrummed in her chest. "You're okay with me and Rennen?" She gave him a searching look and then she saw it, the slight quiver of his jaw muscles. Her heart dropped. No, he wasn't okay with it. He just hated seeing her all torn up. She shook her head. "I appreciate what you're doing, but it won't work."

He cocked his head. "What do you mean?"

"As much as I care about Rennen, I could never live with myself knowing I chose him over you." The words tasted bitter in her mouth.

"You're not choosing him over me," he muttered.

Their eyes locked as she jutted out her chin. "Aren't I? Mom seems to think that's what I've been doing."

He waved a hand. "You know Mom. She's always fired up about something. She'll come to terms with you and Rennen ... eventually."

Ariana got the distinct impression Ace was talking about himself. Tears gathered in her eyes as a wave of tenderness rushed over her. She and Ace had always been close. It meant the world that he would sacrifice his own feelings for her, which is why she had to do the same. There was only one course of action open to her. She released her legs as she angled to face him, keeping her voice light. "I really don't know what the big fuss is about anyway. Rennen and I were just getting to know each other." She chuckled ruefully. "It's not like I'm in love with him, or anything."

Ace blinked. "Oh, my gosh. You are."

She frowned. "What? I just said I wasn't," she spat.

"I know what you said, but I also know what's written all over your face."

She was going to come back with some smart retort, but he held up a hand. "Just hear me out, okay?"

She folded her arms over her chest. "Fine."

"That day at Los Tios when I first learned you were going out with Rennen, I was shocked."

"You mean ticked," she grumbled. She gave him a hard look, daring him to deny it. The wounded look on his face had ripped her to shreds. Heck, her mind still replayed that look over and over.

"Okay, you're right. I was ticked." He paused, his eyes taking on a distant look. "This thing with the Titans had me all tied in knots. I couldn't stand the thought of being replaced, of becoming a has-been."

"Everyone gets replaced eventually," she countered, remembering what Rennen had said. "You were luckier than most. You just ride the wave as long as you can and hope for the best." She was surprised when he smiled.

"That sounds familiar."

"It does?"

"Yeah, Rennen used those same words."

Her heart pounded. "You've been talking to Rennen?"

"Yeah, we spoke earlier today."

"Really?" She tried to wrap her mind around what he was saying. It kind of irked her that Rennen had gone behind her back and talked to Ace ... while she was sitting here eating herself into oblivion. And yet, the notion of Rennen and Ace reaching an understanding sparked more hope in her than she dared express. "What did he say to you?"

"We mostly talked about you."

She rocked back. "Me?"

"Yep."

She clenched her hands. "What did he say?"

A mischievous light came into Ace's eyes. "I can't tell you that. It's against the brotherhood code."

"That's the most absurd thing I've ever heard," she scoffed. "Football players have no brotherhood code."

"It's not about football. This is about men, in general." He chuckled. "But if you must know, Rennen might've said something about me being so fragile that you felt like you had to jump to my defense."

She gritted her teeth. "You wait 'til I get my hands on him."

Ace laughed. "The part about me being fragile is a load of crap," his jaw worked "... mostly. But the part about you jumping to my defense is true."

"I don't feel like I always have to jump to your defense, and I resent Rennen insinuating that I do."

Ace touched his temple, his voice taking on a musing tone. "Let's see. We were in ... Elementary School? Davie Crabtree was picking on me on the playground and before I could even react, you ran up and socked him in the face, bloodying his nose." He shook his head, laughter in his voice. "You barely came to Davie's chest."

Her eyes rounded. "Oh, yeah. I'd forgotten about that." She chuckled, remembering. "Well, he deserved it."

"Yes, he did." His eyes went soft. "I really do appreciate you taking up for me, but I'm a big boy. I had a wonderful career that most players can only dream about. And now I can turn my sights to the restaurants, Silver, Gracie, and the new baby." His eyes went moist. "I have so much to be grateful for. Football was a huge part of my life, but it doesn't define me. At least that's what someone very close to me keeps harping, even gave me two pictures of some silly-looking girls to prove it."

She couldn't help but smile. Ace was referring to the twin pictures she'd given him. Ariana had put them in the guest room of Ace's home, but then little Gracie loved them so much that she wanted them in her bedroom. One picture depicted a poor girl holding a flower. The other a rich girl, also holding a flower. The idea being that both girls had something of value to offer, regardless of their station in life.

"Rich. Poor. Football or no football ... I'm enough." Ace scooted forward. "Look, I know it's awkward for you to be with Rennen ... under the circumstance. But we'll just have to work through it." He gave her a rueful smile. "I have a feeling that you might've finally found your man." He glanced around. "And I think you'd better own up to those feelings before you eat yourself out of house and home ... or at least your clothes."

"Oh, shut up," she said reflexively, then processed his words. Ace was giving her his blessing. Her heart soared, then she frowned. "But what about the press? They'll drag us all through the mud before it's over." She shot him a steely look. "And don't pretend that doesn't bother you, because I know it does."

His jaw tightened. "Yeah, it bothers me." He shrugged. "But what can you do?" His eyes took on a defiant light. "I refuse to live my life tiptoeing around the press."

"Yeah, me too," she said, just now realizing that Ace was right.

He held up a finger, fire sparking in his eyes. "But you can tell your boyfriend that if he has any grand illusions of purchasing a house in The Reserves, he can nix that right now."

Ace referred to the mean-spirited article stating that Rennen was taking everything from Ace and would eventually get his house in The Reserves. She laughed. "I doubt very seriously that Rennen would even want to live in The Reserves. But I'll be sure and tell him."

He looked at the clock. "Don't you have a trip to get ready for?"

She giggled like a sixteen-year-old. "You know about Austin?"

"Yeah, Rennen told me."

She sprang to her feet, hardly believing this was happening. Then as quickly as the excitement came, it faded as her stomach lurched. It was 3:05. "Then you also know Rennen's gone." She could call him and tell him to come back. Yes, that's what she'd do.

Ace stood, a sly smile touching his lips. "You might be surprised."

"You told Rennen you were coming over to talk to me?"

He made a zipping motion over his lips. "Brotherhood code, remember?"

She crossed the distance between them with two steps and flung her arms around her big brother, giving him a tight hug. "Thank you."

"You're welcome." He pulled back, looking her up and down. "You'd better hurry and get dressed. He's gonna be here at 4:00."

A wave of panic raced through her. "He's coming here?" *Yikes!* The place was a disaster. She was a disaster! And she had to pack.

"Yep, that's the plan." Ace wrinkled his nose. "And for goodness' sake, take a shower. You reek of stale chips and Dr. Pepper."

ARIANA HAD JUST GOTTEN DRESSED, her skin still supple from the mist of the shower, when Rennen came to the door. She flung it open—he looked at her, she looked at him—the air crackling with unleashed energy. A soft cry escaped her lips as they rushed into each other's arms. His lips crushed hers with a savage passion as he pulled her closer. A delicious rush wicked through Ariana, making her feel like she was riding a dozen roller coasters all at once. She savored the fire that simmered through her bones as she clung to him, the kiss deepening to the point where she felt their very souls were connecting. This man was filling her heart and soul, taking everything from her, then regenerating it and giving her back impossibly more. She ran her hands over his back, her fingers memorizing the firmness of his sinewy muscles and how they rolled underneath his shirt.

He pulled back, assessing her. "You're amazing."

"So are you," she uttered, getting lost in the depth of his jade, gold eyes—flecks of sunlight on the tips of a lush, green forest.

He searched her face. "For a moment there, I was afraid I'd lost you."

Emotion clogged her throat. "I thought so too," she uttered.

A teasing smile stretched over his lips, lightening the mood. "You taste sweet, like root beer."

Her eyes snapped open, face warming. "Dr. Pepper, actually." *Sheesh.* She'd not yet brushed her teeth. Her breath was probably atrocious. She was grateful she'd thrown away the food wrappers and other incriminating evidence of her carb overload before she jumped in the shower.

Adventure lit his face. "You ready?"

"Almost. I just have to finish packing a few things." *And brush my teeth*, she added mentally.

He stepped away from her and went to the photographs hanging on the wall.

She held her breath, watching him assess them.

He lifted an eyebrow. "These are yours?"

"Yes." The photographs were of landscapes mostly, but one was of her mother and father in the kitchen at Los Tios. She'd caught them in the throes of the dinner hour, their faces glistening with a sheen of sweat, holding platters of food. The picture was one of Ariana's favorites because it captured her parents in motion, a slice of precious time forever preserved.

"These are good." He turned to her, admiration shining in his eyes. "Really good. You're a woman of many talents."

"Thanks," she murmured, a burst of pleasure running through her. She brought her hands together, pulling herself into action. "Well, I'll only be a few more minutes. Make yourself at home."

He nodded, turning his attention back to the photographs, studying them with such intensity that Ariana would've thought they were fine art pieces in a museum rather than simple photographs. It was immensely gratifying to know that Rennen was interested in the things she valued. Excitement brimmed through her as she rushed into her bedroom to finish getting ready for the trip.

11

W hen Rennen and Ariana arrived in Austin the night before, they went straight to the Boyd's home where they had a big birthday party for Gary. Ariana fit right in with the family, and Rennen could tell everyone loved her. They'd spent the night at the Boyd's home and were now standing in the middle of an open field, about to do something Ariana would never forget.

Anticipation rose in Rennen's chest as he glanced at Ariana. Her eyes had sparked like a dozen firecrackers when he announced the big surprise—that he was taking her paramotoring over Austin. Afterwards, they'd drive a little over an hour to spend the remainder of the weekend at a quaint inn in Schulenburg, a German settlement.

Paramotoring was one of Rennen's favorite sports, but paramotoring with Ariana took the experience to a whole new level. He couldn't wait to get her in the air, to share this with her.

Ariana's face was a mask of concentration as she absorbed every word coming out of Warren's mouth. Rennen smiled inwardly as he looked at his best friend who was more like a brother. Warren was giving them the very detailed, lengthy run-through about how to get the paramotor in the air and then land safely. Rennen knew it all like the back of his hand, so he wasn't paying much attention to the instruction.

In high school, Warren had been as much of a jock as Rennen. He was still thin and fit, but his reddish-blonde hair was thinning on top, his skin freckled from a lifetime spent in the harsh Texas sun. Warren was an auto mechanic by trade, but ran a paramotoring school on the side. Warren had gotten into paramotoring when he was in his late teens. Flying had always fascinated Warren, so it was no surprise when he jumped whole-heartedly into the sport. And, of course, it didn't take long for Rennen to get into it as well.

"Paramotoring is essentially paragliding with a motor. It's the same principle as launching a kite. You need opposing air for the glider to lift, which is why you have to run against the wind. Make sure you keep running, even when the glider lifts you," Warren cautioned. "You may run in the air for a couple of seconds, but that's better than the person behind you tripping over you."

Ariana nodded, a determined look on her beautiful face. Even though she was dressed casually in yoga pants and a black t-shirt, her hair was styled, make-up perfect, her diamond-stud earrings glittering in her ears.

"You know why I'm in the back, right?" Rennen asked, keeping a straight face.

Ariana looked thoughtful. "Because you're the expert?"

A grin washed over Rennen's face. "Because I'll cushion your fall if we crash."

She laughed, shoving him. Warren just shook his head, only partially amused. He took his instruction seriously and didn't like Rennen cracking jokes. Rennen glanced at Ariana. "Any confessions you'd like to get off your chest ... in case we don't make it?"

A smile tugged at her lips as her hand went to her hip. "You wish."

"Just saying. When we get up there ... with a single motor ... nothing but air under our feet ... you might be singing a different tune." He knew this would get under Warren's skin, which was why he said it. The two of them got great pleasure out of needling one another.

Warren frowned. "Hey, now. Don't be giving paramotoring a bum rap. It's much safer than flying a small craft."

Ariana made a face. "Really? I wouldn't have thought that."

"Absolutely," Warren continued. "In fact, I feel as safe flying as I do riding a pedal bike in my neighborhood."

"That might be pushing it," Ariana chuckled.

"It's true," Warren argued, red tinging his face.

Rennen laughed. "Oh, no. Don't get him started. Next he'll be spouting off stats."

Ariana cocked her head. "I'd like to hear them. It's fascinating."

Warren shot Rennen a vindicated look. "I'm glad someone appreciates my wisdom."

Rennen only shook his head and smiled.

"Paramotoring is much safer than skydiving," Warren said. "And it's safer than scuba diving."

"Safer than scuba diving?" Ariana wrinkled her nose. "No."

"Four times safer," Warren added. "Just be sure and stay clear of power lines." His light eyes took on a teasing glint as he motioned at Rennen. "Slugger here came gliding down a valley and nearly ran head-on into a string of power lines."

Ariana's eyes widened as she turned to Rennen. "You sure you know what you're doing?"

Rennen cut his eyes at Warren. "Yes, for sure. The incident Warren's referring to happened when I was eighteen. I've gotten a lot more careful with age."

"Let's hope so," Ariana quipped.

Rennen pumped his eyebrows. "You ready?"

A broad smile curved Ariana's lips. "Vamanos."

Warren handed them helmets. "You'll be able to talk to each other through these. They're equipped with radio communication." He looked at Rennen. "How long are you planning on staying up? You have enough gas for about two hours."

"We'll probably stay up for a good hour ... maybe a little more," Rennen said. "The plan is to come back to this spot."

"All right. Sounds good. I've got a few errands to run then I'll come back here to wait for you."

A BREATHLESS EXCITEMENT came over Ariana, partly because they were about to lift into the air and partly because Rennen was so close. It was fun being here with him and seeing the playful banter between Rennen and the Boyds. It reminded Ariana a little of her own family. This was a side of Rennen she'd not seen and she liked it. He was more carefree and open here.

"You ready?" Rennen asked through the radio.

"Yep."

He started the engine. "Let's do it. Run like the wind."

Ariana ran as hard as she could, keenly aware that her fastest pace was probably excruciatingly slow for Rennen. She hated feeling like the weak link in the operation. She felt the glider pull up behind them. And as Warren said, she kept running even when she felt them lift. Her stomach swooped as they rose in the air. Then came the rush of exhilaration.

"How ya doing?" Rennen asked.

"Great," she breathed. Then realized she was yelling into the mic. As they lifted higher, the field below became a tiny square of green. The landscape unfolded before their eyes. Ariana took everything in, feeling like she could see forever. "This has to be one of the coolest things I've ever done," she murmured.

"I'm glad you like it," Rennen said, appreciation coating his voice.

Being up here with Rennen made her feel as free as a bird soaring in the air without a care in the world.

"Look to your left," Rennen said.

"Wow." Her gaze took in Austin's cityscape with a large cluster of buildings that looked like rectangle boxes from their altitude. The trees were tiny green circles. The view was similar to what you'd see from an airplane, but there was a weightlessness with only the air around them. Ariana could see how paramotoring could get in your blood. Her eye caught on a ribbon of blue from the lake snaking around the perimeter of the city. Extending out from that were neat rows of homes reminding Ariana of houses in the board game Monopoly, except they were beige instead of green. Everything looked so orderly and pristine up here, the landscape cut into intricate sections of browns, greens, and blues.

Ariana lost track of time as they flew higher. The sky above was a bright, azure blue with tufts of wispy clouds. She felt like she was in the middle of a splendid dream. It was hard to believe she was here with Rennen ... and that nothing was stopping them from being together.

"Uh, oh."

It was astounding how quickly those two words struck fear in Ariana's heart as she tightened her grip on the rope handles, level with her head. "What's wrong?"

"The motor's cutting out."

It coughed and sputtered, jerking them in the process.

Ariana looked down at the ground, which seemed a world away. Whereas she'd felt free before, she now felt exposed and vulnerable —a tiny dot with nothing but menacing air around them. If they plummeted to the ground, there would be nothing left of them.

The motor died.

Rennen swore. "That's not good."

A suffocating silence pressed around them. And then they started to drop.

Ariana gasped, her life flashing before her eyes. A heavy fear thudded in her chest, stealing her breath. She didn't want to die. Not when she'd just found Rennen. She thought of her family and how much she loved them. It stabbed through her heart to think she'd never see them again. Then it occurred to Ariana that she'd not yet told Rennen how she felt about him. She'd only just realized the full scope of her feelings the previous day when Ace pointed it out to her. *All in or nothing.* "I love you," she blurted.

"What?"

She heard the surprise in his voice, but she had to get it all out while she still could. "I know we've only known each other for a short period of time. But the time we've spent together has been the greatest of my life." Tears rolled down her cheeks as she gripped the handles so hard her hands hurt.

"Are you okay?"

She belted out an incredulous laugh. "Well, considering I'm staring death in the face, I guess I'm doing all right. I'm glad we got a chance to meet. I was beginning to think I'd never find you. You just don't know how long I've searched for you." A heavy sorrow settled in the pit of her stomach. "I'm only sorry it happened too late." Rennen made a noise. At first, her mind didn't comprehend what the sound was. Then she realized he was laughing. Hurt splintered through her and with it came an acrid anger. "You're laughing at me?"

"I guess you really did have a lot to get off your chest."

"We're dying, and you're laughing at me?" she yelled through the radio receiver. *Of all the inconsiderate, lousy things to do.* "Jerk!"

"We're not dying. We're coasting in for a landing."

"W-what?" The relief that pelted through her made her dizzy. "But the engine ..."

"Yeah, the stupid thing's dead as a doornail, for sure. Warren should've spent as much time checking his equipment as he did giving us pointers. But we're not gonna die. I was planning on circling back so we could land in the same field where we took off, but we'll have to land somewhere else. It'll be a bit of a drive for Warren, but he can pick us up."

Heat burned Ariana's cheeks and yet she couldn't help but feel overjoyed. They weren't going to die. A hesitant laugh bubbled out. "Oops. I guess I let the cat out of the bag, huh?"

Rennen let out a deep, throaty chuckle. "Yeah, but it's okay. I won't hold it against you."

Won't hold it against me? This is where he was supposed to tell her he loved her too. When he remained silent, her heart flopped like a dead fish on dry land. Humiliation burned through her veins. She did love Rennen, but it was too soon in their relationship to say it out loud—too soon to spill her guts. *Great.* Now he'd think she was crazy ... and desperate.

Silence descended between them like a mile-high wall, impossible to climb. As they drifted down to earth, Rennen tugged on the handles, maneuvering them to an open field. The ground loomed large at their feet, until finally, they touched down. When they stepped out of the harnesses, Ariana was consumed with a hot embarrassment. She hardly dared look at Rennen. Then again, she was no coward. She steeled her shoulders. For better or worse, she'd opened up her heart and it was up to him to decide what to do with it.

Rennen pumped a fist in the air and let out a whoop. "That was awesome!"

"Yeah, it was great," she said flatly.

Amusement lit his eyes, turning his gold flecks to streaks of sunlight over a fathomless pond as he stepped up to her. "So, you love me."

She scowled. "Don't let it go to your head, Goldie Locks."

He chuckled. "Sorry, I didn't mean to laugh up there. You just caught me off guard."

"Well, I'm glad I could add to your amusement," she responded tartly.

His gaze roved over her like he was photographing her features. She was about to say something about it when he slid a hand around her waist, pulling her roughly to him. "I'm glad you love me," he said, a quirky grin slipping over his lips.

She rested the flats of her palms against his chest, trying not to notice the definition of his muscles. "Oh, yeah?" She gave him an icy glare. "Why's that?"

"Because I love you too."

She gulped. "You do?" She certainly wasn't expecting that. She searched his rugged face, craving reassurance.

"Absolutely," he drawled, eyes smoldering with desire. His lips crushed hers in a demanding kiss that licked fire through her blood, sending delicious quivers rippling through her. His hands moved up her back to her neck where he buried his fingers in her hair. A groan rumbled in her throat as she soared back up to the clouds in a mist of sheer bliss.

FROM WHAT RENNEN COULD TELL, they were about thirty-five miles from their point of origin. The average flight speed was twenty-five miles an hour with no wind, and they'd been traveling for about an hour and fifteen minutes. He pulled out his phone and did a check on Google Maps. Yep, that was about right. He called Warren. "Hey, it's me."

"Are you on your way back?"

"No, the engine died on us."

"Aw, man. Are you serious?"

"Yep."

"Sorry about that. It must be the spark plugs. They've been giving me problems. Did it sputter before dying?"

"Sure did." Rennen couldn't help but smile. It had certainly worked in his favor. Ariana felt his gaze and smiled. Then she stretched her legs and leaned back, lifted her face to the sun. They were sitting in a field in the middle of nowhere, about ten yards from a country road.

"Where are you?"

"Driftwood. According to Google Maps, we're near Elder Hill Road."

"All right. I'll check your location in my Friend Finder App. Hang tight. I'll be there as soon as I can."

Rennen shoved his phone in his pocket and lay back. Ariana scooted next to him and rested her head on his chest. Rennen was on top of the world, still flying high. It was crazy how quickly things could change. Yesterday, he'd felt like Ariana was slipping away. Out of sheer desperation, he'd called Ace and asked him to meet at a coffee shop so they could talk things over. Ace had been cool and distant at first. Then Rennen grew frustrated and accused Ace of being a self-centered putz who was more concerned about his own image than his sister's happiness. For a second, Rennen thought Ace might punch him, but then Ace started laughing. "You really care about my sister, don't you?"

"Yeah, I care," he shot back. "Enough to come here and plead with you to put her first. You had your moment to shine on the field, and I'm having mine. Eventually, someone else will have his. But this goes beyond that. This is about me and Ariana. A woman like her comes along once in a lifetime, and I'm not willing to give her up for anyone or anything."

It was then that Ace looked at him through new eyes, and the conversation shifted. Rennen didn't hold any grand illusions of him and Ace becoming bosom buds. But at least they'd reached an understanding, enough for Ace to give Ariana the green light to come with him to Austin.

"How long will it take for Warren to get here?" Ariana craned her neck to look at him.

"Probably about forty-five minutes."

She grinned. "Good. Enough time to take a nap."

"A nap sounds good." A feeling of contentment settled over Rennen. It felt right to have Ariana here with him. The warmth of the sun felt good. Thankfully, it wasn't as hot as it normally was in June— maybe in the mid-eighties as opposed to the nineties. Rennen was almost asleep when his phone buzzed. He didn't want to answer it. He just wanted to lay here and relax.

"Maybe you should get that," Ariana said, her voice lazy. "It might be Warren."

He sighed. "You're probably right." He sat up, forcing Ariana to sit up in the process. He fished his phone out of his jeans. It was Lainey Summerfield from DaVinici PR Firm. She'd called a few times, but he hadn't gotten around to returning her call. He thought about letting it go to voicemail, but decided to go ahead and answer it, so the woman wouldn't keep pestering him.

"Hello."

"Rennen," she began briskly, "I've been trying to reach you."

"Yeah, sorry. Things have been a little hectic. What's up?"

"I wanted to go over the particulars of the upcoming rematch with Ariana Sanchez. As we've already discussed, the plan is for it to be held on the practice field of the Titan Sports Complex at 2:00 p.m. one week from this coming Tuesday."

"Okay. Sounds good."

"I still need to confirm that time with Miss Sanchez. And then we'll notify the media."

Rennen glanced at Ariana who was watching him. "I can ask Ariana right now."

"She's there with you?" Lainey blustered.

"Yep. Hold on." He lowered the phone. "It's Lainey Summerfield from DaVinici. She wants to know if it's okay with you to hold the rematch a week from Tuesday at 2:00 p.m.?" It was cute the way color seeped into Ariana's cheeks as her eyes widened. "Are we still going through with the rematch ... now that we're ... together?"

He chuckled. "Of course. You still want the money, don't you?"

"Well, yeah. I was gonna use it to renovate the gym. And I want the donation to go to the charity."

"All right. It's settled. Is that time okay with you?"

She shrugged, a sly grin tugging at her lips. "Yeah, if you're still good with getting your butt whipped on national TV."

He laughed. "That's yet to be determined." He put the phone to his mouth. "A week from Tuesday works for us. And 2:00 is fine." No response. "Lainey, are you still there?"

"Yes, I'm here."

"Oh, I thought I'd lost you for a minute. Did you hear what I said? We're good on the date and time."

"Are you and Ariana Sanchez a couple?"

His chest expanded with pride as he gave Ariana a tender smile. "Yep, we're officially a couple."

Ariana's face turned even redder, but she smiled like she was glad he was calling it.

"Is that a good idea?" Lainey asked, her voice dripping with disapproval. "I thought we decided that should anything develop between you and Ariana, you were going to wait until after the rematch to make it official."

When the article came out about Rennen and Ariana kissing at the climbing gym, it had left the DaVinici Firm scrambling to figure out how to respond to the accusation that James Knight was using the rematch to deflect negative publicity from Hailey Knight and Brady Giles. Not to mention the fact that Anthony Kincaid was particularly evasive about talking to the press about his injury last year.

A deep furrow creased his forehead. "I don't see a problem with releasing the information now. It's the truth, after all." Ariana gave him a puzzled look, to which he forced a smile.

"I don't think you realize all the problems it will cause if the press thinks you and Ariana are in cahoots. They might assume you staged the whole thing for the publicity and the money."

The hair on Rennen's neck bristled. "I don't care what the press assumes."

Ariana's face tightened as she gave him a questioning look. He offered a reassuring smile as he put a hand on her arm.

"Mr. Bradley, you hired us to protect your image, and that's what we're trying to do. But you have to cooperate."

He clenched his jaw, his blood pumping faster. Lainey only called him by his last name when she was ticked. Well, she'd just have to get over it. Rennen was ticked that everyone kept trying to dictate how he should live his life. "Ariana and I are a couple. And I don't care who knows it. I'll shout it from the rooftops. My job is to live my life how I see fit, and your job is to manage the fallout. You got that?" he growled.

"Loud and clear, sir."

Lainey's sarcasm wasn't lost on him, but he decided to let it go. "Will there be anything else?"

Long pause.

"Are you there?" Rennen asked, gripping the phone.

"Yes, there is one other thing. I had hoped to have this conversation in person," Lainey said stiffly. "But since you're never available …

we need to come up with a plan in the event one of the parental claims should happen to be legitimate."

A hard laugh scratched out of Rennen's throat. "I told you, Lainey. I'm not interested in any claim, legitimate or not." Ariana was studying him with concern. He tried to smile to smooth out the situation, but it came out feeling more like a grimace.

Lainey sighed heavily. "Yes, I know that's what you keep saying. But you just can't turn your back on this and hope it'll go away. Because it won't," she added, her voice ringing with conviction. "If someone comes forward with viable information about your past, it's better to keep the channel open so they'll come to us first. Then we can mitigate it."

Blood was pounding in Rennen's temples and he felt like he wanted to punch something. "No!" he almost shouted.

"If you'll just give it some thought."

"I don't need to give it more thought," he roared. "My answer is final."

"But, Rennen—"

"Goodbye." He ended the call.

Ariana studied him. "Are you okay?"

He let out a breath. "Yeah."

"What kind of claim were you talking about? A parental claim?"

"Yes." He rubbed a hand across his forehead. "My PR rep thinks it's in my best interest to come up with a plan in case a legitimate claim comes forward." The words cut leaving his mouth. He hated how his past was being dredged up and that he even had to think about this.

Ariana searched his face. "I hate to say this, but she may have a point."

He let out a humorless laugh. "Not you too."

She touched his arm. "Once you learn about your past, then you can put it behind you for good."

"I've already put it behind me," he barked. "I don't give a crap who my parents were."

Ariana arched an eyebrow, probing him with her perceptive eyes.

"What?"

"I think you do care."

"That's ridiculous," he scoffed.

"In fact, I think you care a lot, which is why you're so defensive."

"No, you're wrong. I don't care. I've done everything on my own." He balled his fist. "And no one's gonna come around now, trying to get a piece of it." He couldn't let this mess with his head. He had to remain strong, just as he'd always done.

Sparks lit her eyes. "You're assuming that people who come forward want your money and fame. But what if that's not true? It's possible that someone's really trying to find you."

A disbelieving laugh rose in his throat. "Yeah, and it's possible that pigs fly."

Her brows drew together, creasing her forehead. "Or maybe your parents are louses. But at least you'll know the truth so you can get closure on it."

The words broke loose like a dam giving way to a raging river. "I know you mean well. But you have no idea what it's like to be abandoned—to be left alone to fend for yourself. No one caring if you have enough food to eat. No one caring if you live or die." He pointed to his chest. "Well, I do. I learned a long time ago that the only person I could depend on was me."

Ariana jerked back, a wounded look on her face.

"That didn't come out right." He let out a deflated breath. The last thing he wanted to do was argue with her. Today was supposed to be fun—a day to celebrate them being together. "I'm sorry. I didn't mean that I can't depend on you. I was speaking metaphorically, trying to make you understand how I feel." He hated the emotion building inside him. Hated that a small part of him did care who his parents were ... even after all this time.

He sucked in a ragged breath as they eyed one another. Finally, Ariana's features softened and she gave him a tiny smile. "You're right. I can't begin to understand what you've been through." Her eyes took on a pleading look. "I know you're angry and you have a right to be." Her voice caught. "But that anger's not hurting your parents. It's festering inside of you—you're the one who's getting ripped to shreds. That's why you need to let it go."

"I can't," he slung back. His anger had made him strong ... had been the only thing he could hold onto. He shook his head. "I'm sorry." He expected her to react in anger and was surprised ... relieved when he saw understanding in her eyes.

She cupped his face. "It'll be okay."

He nodded. "I know it will be." He placed a hand over hers. "Now that I have you."

"Yes, you do." A full smile broke over her face. "And I'm not going anywhere."

Ariana had no idea how much it meant to hear those words.

"So," she drawled. "I take it your PR rep's not too happy about us being official, huh?"

He scowled. "Sorry you had to hear that. The whole thing's ridiculous."

"With all the pictures of us together, it's not like it's a big surprise. Why is she upset about it?"

"Because she's afraid it'll take thunder away from our rematch. If we're together already, then the press won't find it nearly as entertaining." He didn't dare mention the part about them looking like they were doing it solely for the money. Ariana wouldn't react well to that.

Her eyes widened. "Seriously?"

"Seriously."

"I don't care if the whole dang world knows we're a couple," he said.

She laughed. "Me either. Now that Ace is okay with it."

They jumped when they heard a horn. A black Lexus pulled along the side of the road. The passenger window rolled down. A man was driving with a woman in the passenger seat. From what Rennen could tell, they both looked to be in their mid-fifties or early sixties.

"Hello," the woman said pleasantly. "It looks like you could use some help."

Rennen offered a friendly smile and wave. "Thanks, but we're doing okay."

"That gear looks interesting. What were you doing?" the woman asked.

"Curious, aren't they?" Ariana muttered under her breath.

Rennen was amused. "We're out in the country. Everyone's curious." He looked at Ariana, a wicked grin tugging at his lips.

"What?" she whispered.

"My girlfriend and I were paramotoring," he said loudly to the woman. "Until our engine died."

"What're you up to?" Ariana demanded, tugging on his arm.

"Proclaiming my love to the world." He looked at the woman. "In case you were wondering, my name's Rennen Bradley, and I'm in love with Ariana Sanchez," he boomed.

The woman in the car chuckled. "Nice to know. Would you like a ride into town?"

"No, thank you," Rennen said. "We're waiting for a friend to pick us up."

"Are you sure?" the woman asked.

"Yes, but thank you."

The woman looked like she might say something else, but smiled instead. "Okay, if you're sure."

"Yep, very sure," Rennen chimed.

"Have a great day," the woman said. "Nice meeting you, Rennen Bradley, and your girlfriend." There was a trace of mirth in her voice.

Rennen offered a parting wave. "Thanks."

The woman nodded as she rolled up her window and they drove away.

Ariana shoved him. "You're such a dork."

"I can't help it if I'm totally and completely in love with you," he uttered.

Her eyes danced. "Ditto." She cocked her head. "She seemed nice."

"Who? The woman? Yes, she did," Rennen agreed.

"Do you think she recognized you?"

He shrugged. "I really don't care. I'm tired of living my life in fear of the press."

"Me too." She paused. "I'm glad there are still good people in the world who are willing to lend a helping hand to strangers."

Rennen hadn't thought about it that way, but it was a good point. "Yeah, me too." He drew her close. "I'm glad I have you in my world."

Her features softened into a smile. "And I'm glad I have you. It works nicely."

"Yes, it does," he murmured, leaning in for a kiss.

12

Nestled on a quaint corner of historical Schulenburg, The Hideaway Inn looked like something out of a storybook with the large, circular, twin porches on each side of the front door. Ariana's gaze took in the bay windows with intricate leaded-glass on the top sections. Decorative trim added the finishing touches, and the siding glistened like fresh milk in the afternoon sun. The landscape boasted an explosion of colorful flowers—some in pots and others popping up from the ground.

"What do you think?"

The hope shining on Rennen's face caused a rush of tenderness to come over her. She smiled broadly. "It's perfect."

"Let's take our luggage in and get settled, then I'll show you around the town. We may even be able to tour one of the painted churches ... if they're not already closed for the day." He pumped his eyebrows. "That is, unless you'd rather go to the Polka Music Museum instead. I know how much you love dancing."

She laughed. "Yeah, but Polka?" She wrinkled her forehead. "I think I'll pass in favor of the churches."

He grinned, his eyes teasing. "That's probably wise. A little religion will keep you on the straight and narrow."

"Hey, now. Watch it." She nudged him, thrusting out her lower lip. But she couldn't stop a laugh from rolling in her throat. With Rennen, there was never a dull moment. She had to keep pinching herself to make sure this was really happening. Her heart sang as she reached for her bags and followed him up the steps. On the drive from Austin to Schulenburg, Rennen told her a little about the place where they'd be spending the night.

The town was settled in the 1800s by German immigrants who'd left Europe to escape poverty. While these people embraced their new life in America, they brought parts of their culture with them. The churches were decorated with colors and symbols from their homelands. Rennen explained that there were fifteen of these churches scattered throughout Texas, four of them near Schulenburg.

It was fascinating to hear Rennen expound on the history of the area. She could tell from listening to him that he was wicked smart. Yes, he may've grown up in hard circumstances, but it certainly hadn't hindered his ability to excel. Another thought struck her. Maybe Rennen was so strong because of the hardships he'd endured.

As they stepped through the front door of the inn, Ariana took in the foyer with the plush Oriental rug and round, walnut table in the center. A large floral arrangement set atop it. The room opened to a gorgeous staircase that curved on both sides where it touched the floor like the train of a gown. Ariana peered into the adjacent sitting room with curved-backed furniture and a baby grand piano nestled in the pocket of the bay windows. The room was cozy and in-keeping with the period.

Directly across from the sitting room was a library with floor to ceiling shelves of books. In the center was an arrangement of plush, leather furniture. A fireplace took up the center section of one wall. Over the mantle was a large oil painting of a family dressed in clothes from the early 1900s. Ariana felt like they'd stepped back in time. Her eye caught on the burgundy afghan draped across the back of the sofa. The room was so inviting that it made Ariana want to snuggle up with a good book and wile away the afternoon.

They walked over to the reception desk and Rennen rang the bell. A couple of minutes later, a short man with thinning hair and a round belly came trotting towards them, the wood floor creaking underneath his feet. A large smile lit his ruddy face, causing his mustache to twitch. "Welcome."

"Thank you," Rennen and Ariana replied simultaneously.

He stepped behind the desk and pushed his glasses back up on his nose. "What's the name?"

"Rennen Bradley."

He punched keys on the computer, staring at the screen. A second later, he looked at Rennen. "You booked two adjoining rooms, is that correct?"

"Yes."

It was evident that the man didn't recognize Rennen, which was a good thing. They could enjoy their privacy. Ariana stepped closer to Rennen and linked her arm through his. He'd gone to a lot of trouble to make sure their weekend was perfect. She was so glad she'd come.

"Wonderful," the man said. "Your rooms are ready. Dinner is served in the dining room from six to nine." He pointed. "At the end of the hall to the right. You can also go out on the veranda. We have a live band playing tonight. Breakfast is served in the morning ... also from six to nine a.m." He chuckled. "It helps keep things simple so there's no confusion in this old brain." He handed Rennen two keys. "Your rooms are on the second floor." He pointed to the staircase. "Turn right, go down the hall to the last two rooms on the right. Both have their own bathrooms. My name's Walter. If you need anything, don't hesitate to call the front desk. There are phones in your rooms. Just dial zero."

"Will do," Rennen said.

Ariana smiled at Walter. "Thanks." When they reached the top of the stairs, Ariana turned to Rennen, looking up into his eyes. "This place is fantastic. A quaint dinner ... live band. You're pulling out all the stops. I might have to rethink my position on football players."

He cocked an eyebrow in amusement. "Is that so?"

She laughed. "Or at least one football player." She rolled her eyes.

"Of course, you did trick me into thinking I was dying and spilling my guts."

A quirky grin tugged at his lips. "Yeah, it might take you a while to live that one down."

"For sure."

"I'm glad you like the inn. I've always wanted to stay here."

She cocked her head. "You've never been here before? You're so familiar with the town. I just assumed ..."

"Nope. First time." He grinned, his eyes shining. "And we get to experience it together."

"Oh, didn't I tell you? I've stayed here before." She had to fight to keep from breaking into laughter when she saw his shocked expression. He was so much fun to tease. "Just kidding. I've never been here before. This is a wonderful first."

He leaned closer, his eyes turning a deep, moss green as he looked at her lips. "Well, here's to firsts."

A smile overtook her lips. "Indeed."

———

SOFT LIGHT from the candle on the table flickered against Ariana's features, giving her an air of mystery. Rennen drank in her beauty as he leaned forward and reached for her hands. "It's so nice to be here with you." She was wearing a purple dress that hit her figure in all the right places—her tiny waist, leading down to her curvy hips and toned legs. Silver earrings dangled underneath her hair, capturing the light with every movement. Rennen had never seen a woman look so spectacular. She literally took his breath away.

A playful grin touched her full lips. "What? You keep staring at me."

"Because you're stunning."

She rewarded him with a dazzling smile. "You're not so bad yourself, Goldie Locks."

Music from the live band floated on the evening air—a contemporary jazz song that fit perfectly with the evening. Tomorrow morning, Rennen and Ariana planned to attend a sunrise service at the church they'd toured. Then they'd drive back to Ft. Worth, stopping for lunch along the way. This trip had been the perfect escape from all the craziness. No one had recognized them. Here, they were simply a couple in love. Rennen wasn't looking forward to going back into the lion's den, but they'd have to face it sooner or later. At least now, they could face it together.

Now, they sat on the back veranda of the inn, waiting to order their dinner. The evening sky was awash with orange and blue swirls from the setting sun. A girl in her late teens approached their table. "Hello, my name's Mindy. And I'll be taking care of you tonight."

They placed their drink orders—Rennen water with lemon, and Ariana a Dr. Pepper.

"Would you like any appetizers?" Mindy asked.

Rennen leaned back in his seat. "What do you recommend?"

"The bruschetta is good. As is the calamari."

Rennen looked at Ariana. "What do you think?"

"They both sound delicious."

He nodded. "Yes, they do. We'll have both."

Mindy smiled. "Perfect. I'll put this in and be right back to take your dinner orders."

Ariana gave him a questioning look. "Two appetizers?"

"I figure we're celebrating so we can splurge a little."

She laughed. "Sure. Why not. I've eaten enough the past couple of days to kill a cow. We'll just have to exercise more next week."

He chuckled. "Amen."

Rennen picked up the menu. "What're you getting?"

Ariana pursed her lips as she perused the menu. "The crab cakes look good. How about you? What're you thinking?"

"A steak and loaded baked potato."

"Simple and direct. I like that." She winked. "I knew you were a meat and potatoes man at heart."

"Yeah, but I like a lot of different types of food."

Her eyes sparkled in a challenge. "How do you feel about Mexican food?"

"Hate it," he said with a straight face.

She gave him a steely look. "You're lying."

He broke into a smile. "Yeah, you're right."

"I've got your number." She wagged a finger. "If you're gonna be a part of my family, you've got to like Mexican food."

He leaned forward, locking eyes with her. "Part of your family ... I like the sound of that." For a second, he thought he might've spoken out of turn, but it didn't seem to bother Ariana. Things were happening fast between them, but he couldn't deny that it felt right. He kept replaying the words Ariana had spoken when she thought they were going to crash. She said she'd been looking for him her entire life. He knew she meant that she'd been looking for someone like him, but the meaning was sort of the same. It felt good to be needed.

"I guess the true test of our relationship will come after you meet my family," Ariana joked.

"From what you said, your mother seems like quite the character."

"Oh, she is. Believe me. She's like this big, bright shining star in the center of the room that must be paid attention to. But she's got a heart of gold." She laughed to herself. "She's been pestering me to find a good guy and settle down, especially now that Ace found Silver."

He reached for her hand, locking gazes with her. "And have you?" It was fun to watch the color that crept into her cheeks.

"Have I what?" she asked, even though she knew exactly what he was asking.

"Found a good guy to settle down with."

The sincerity in her eyes was like invisible hands that reached out and pulled him close to her with some indefinable bond. "I sure hope so," she said wistfully.

Her answer confused him, jolted him a little. He forced a laugh, trying to keep the hurt out of his voice. "You hope so?"

"Yeah, I believe we have something unique ... something that only comes along once in a lifetime ... I guess time's the trump card, right?"

"Yeah, I guess."

Her dark eyes searched his. "I want us to work. Want it more than air," she said fervently. "But we've only just met."

Was she retreating? She'd professed her love for him earlier, and he assumed they were a done deal. Then again, nothing was set in stone. He didn't know why he was getting upset about semantics. Ariana was telling him she wanted to be with him. A couple of days ago, he was trying to get her to spend the weekend with him. Now they were moving forward as a couple. He needed to be satisfied with that. He wished he could banish the insecurity gnawing at the back of his mind. "You're right," he said, when he realized she was watching him, waiting for an answer. "We'll take things one step at a time." He grinned as he said it, feeling a little better.

She smiled back in relief.

He was hungry to know everything about her. "I've been thinking about those photos in your living room."

Pleasure lit her face. "Really?"

"Do you always shoot black and white?"

She tucked a strand of hair behind her ear. "Not always. But I do prefer black and white. It lends a timeless quality to the photo."

"I can see that. Kind of like it's been there forever."

"Yeah, and will last forever."

The intense look in her eyes got him right in the heart. She was talking about the two of them. He felt his confidence being restored. Whenever something good happened to Rennen, he had a tendency to wait for the other shoe to drop. He was trying to break himself of that habit, but a lifetime of conditioning was hard to overcome. He realized Ariana was still talking about her photography.

"There's a purity about black and white that I really like. Color can sometimes distract from the true meaning of the story. When you strip away the superfluous, you're left with what really matters."

A smile tugged at his lips. "Kind of like getting away from our hectic lives and coming here."

She laughed lightly. "Exactly."

"What kind of music do you like?"

She cocked her head. "You're asking a lot of questions."

"Because I want to know everything about you."

"I like most types of music. Jazz, rock ... some country." A smile played on her lips. "Even mariachi music. I am Mexican, after all."

"No. Hmm," he drawled. "I may have to rethink this."

She shook her head, delicate laughter floating up from her throat. "You know what they say, ain't no skin like Mex-skin."

He laughed in surprise. "That's pretty good." Rennen didn't think of Ariana as being Mexican, per se. It was just a part of who she was.

"How about you? What types of music do you like?"

"Rock, country, jazz." The corners of his mouth quivered. "Polka."

She burst out laughing. "I knew we should've gone to that Polka museum today."

He snapped his fingers. "Dang it. We missed our big chance."

"Oh, well. There's always next time, right?"

A blanket of warmth spread over him as he saw the promise in her eyes. They'd have a lifetime of tomorrows together. "Right," he said exuberantly. The air around them crackled with electricity as their eyes connected. Rennen wished they were alone so he could pull Ariana into his arms and kiss her until they couldn't see straight.

"Well, hello again," a cheery voice said, interrupting the moment.

Rennen looked up at the man and woman walking toward them. At first, he didn't recognize them. Then he remembered—the couple from the black Lexus. "Hey." He rose to his feet and extended a hand. "Good to see you again."

The woman gave him a firm shake as she smiled, the skin around her eyes folding into deep creases. "Likewise, Rennen Bradley." She turned to Ariana, "And his beautiful girlfriend. Ariana Sanchez, wasn't it?"

Recognition registered on Ariana's face as she smiled. "Oh, you're the couple who saw us today in the field. Hello ... again."

Rennen looked past the woman to the man standing behind her. The woman motioned. "This is Thomas."

He extended his hand, shaking Ariana's first, then Rennen's.

The woman pointed to herself. "My name is Della Chastain. What a coincidence that we'd run into you twice in one day."

"Yes, it is a coincidence." Rennen gave her a direct look. "Are you staying here ... in the inn?" Considering how reporters bombarded him at every turn, he was always suspicious of coincidences.

"Yes, we are. Thomas's sister lives in Driftwood, just a few miles from where we saw you in the field. Tomorrow, we're headed to San Antonio to see the Riverwalk and Alamo. We figured since we were out this way, we might as well do some sightseeing."

"Oh, that's nice." Rennen felt a little guilty for being suspicious. Della and Thomas were a classy couple, not the reporter types. Her blonde hair, streaked with silver, rounded on her shoulders. Intelligent eyes peered out from behind stylish glasses. Her makeup was expertly applied and Rennen could tell she'd had quite a bit of cosmetic work done, but it was tasteful. Thomas had closely-cropped, silvery-white hair with watery blue eyes and patrician features. Both looked like they'd come from money and influence.

"I'm glad to see that your friend did indeed pick you up. I felt so bad leaving you stranded on the side of the road," Della said.

Now that Rennen was right next to Della, he picked up on her New York accent ... or at least that's how she sounded to him. He waved the apology away. "Warren showed up about twenty minutes after you left." He glanced at Ariana who didn't look very happy to have their dinner interrupted.

Della shifted like she was suddenly uncomfortable. "I hate to ask you this, but would you mind if we ate dinner with you tonight?"

When he saw Ariana's eyes bulge, Rennen laughed inwardly. He felt exactly the same way. It lay on the tip of his tongue to tell Della *no*.

Della laughed nervously. "All of the other tables are taken." She glanced over her shoulder. "Except for the one, but that poor couple has their hands full."

Rennen followed her trail of vision to the table across from them. A young mother and father were having a hard time getting their kids under control. The baby was crying and the toddler running around the table, squealing. He couldn't help but chuckle inwardly. He didn't blame Della and Thomas for not wanting to sit there. He looked to Ariana for approval. She seemed to be reading his thoughts as her features softened.

"Of course you can join us," Ariana said, flashing an accommodating smile.

Rennen shot her a look of appreciation, to which she nodded slightly in acknowledgement.

Della and Thomas sat down. "Thanks so much," Della said. "We're sorry to intrude on your evening."

"It's okay." Rennen forced a smile. "It's always nice to meet new folks."

Mindy returned with the drinks and appetizers. She looked at Della and Thomas in surprise. "Oh, I didn't realize you had other people joining you."

"Yes," Ariana explained. "There weren't any tables open so they're sitting with us."

Mindy frowned. "It has been busy tonight." She paused. "But there are other tables available on the backside of the terrace. You just have to walk around the corner. Most people don't realize they're there."

Della's eyes widened as she chuckled sheepishly. "Oh, we didn't even see those, did we Thomas?"

He shook his head, a deep blush coming over his pale skin. "No. We just looked in the dining room and then came out here and everything was full."

"If you'd like, I can take you to another table," Mindy offered.

A look passed between Della and Thomas. "I think we're good here," Della said quickly. She looked at Rennen and Ariana. "If you're okay. Thomas and I eat alone all the time. It's nice to have some company."

Rennen looked at Ariana. It would be downright rude to turn away this nice couple. And yet, the situation was awkward.

"We're fine if you stay," Ariana said.

That had the magical effect of soothing the tension as Della and Thomas got comfortable in their seats.

"I'll bring a couple more menus," Mindy said, "and more place settings."

"They can use our menus. Ariana and I already know what we want to order." Rennen passed his menu to Della as Ariana did the same to Thomas. They placed their drink orders.

Rennen motioned. "Please, help yourself to the appetizers. We ordered extra."

After the food orders were placed and Mindy collected the menus, Della turned to Rennen, interest simmering in her eyes. "So, tell me about what you were doing today. I can't remember what you said it was called."

"Paramotoring," Rennen answered.

Thomas held up a finger. "Yes, that's right ... paramotoring."

Della cocked her head. "I've heard of paragliding but not paramotoring."

Rennen took a bite of bruschetta, his tongue tingling from the tanginess of the fresh tomatoes. "They're very similar, except one has a motor."

Ariana scooped a generous portion of calamari onto her plate, her voice bubbling with amusement. "And if the motor happens to die in flight, you can glide to the ground. I learned that the hard way today." She looked at Rennen as she spoke.

Rennen relished the intimate connection that flowed between them.

"You mentioned something about your motor dying today, but I didn't know what you meant." Della looked mortified. "I'll bet that was scary."

"Petrifying," Ariana added. "I thought we were gonna die."

Della turned to Ariana. "Do you go paramotoring often?"

"Nope. Today was my first time. Rennen does though. He grew up doing it."

All eyes turned to Rennen. "I've been paramotoring since I was a teenager," he explained. "My best friend Warren got me into it."

"He's the friend who was picking you up today," Della said.

"Yep."

Mindy returned with Della and Thomas's drinks and brought Rennen and Ariana refills.

Rennen looked at Della. "Where are you from? I detect a New York Accent."

She looked impressed. "Yes, Thomas and I are from the Hamptons."

Della was definitely the talker of the two. Thomas seemed content to sit back and let her steer the conversation. "How about you and Ariana? Are you from this area?"

Rennen held back, thinking Ariana might want to answer, but when she remained silent, he took that as a cue to continue. "We're from the Dallas/Ft. Worth Area."

Della nodded, glancing at Thomas, a look passing between them. She reached for her water and took a long drink. Then she let out a hesitant laugh. "I wouldn't feel right without telling you that after we saw you in the field today ... and you announced your name ... we thought it sounded familiar. We looked you up. Then it all clicked. I remember seeing you on the Katie Moss interview."

Rennen's jaw tightened as he nodded. Now he knew why they'd wanted to sit with him and Ariana—to rub shoulders with a NFL player. Disappointment weighted his stomach.

"Don't worry," Della assured him, lowering her voice. "We won't say a word to the other guests."

"We appreciate that," Ariana said. "We came here to get some privacy."

Rennen heard the slight jab in Ariana's tone, knew it was directed at Della and Thomas for forcing their way into this dinner. Still, they seemed harmless. Rennen relaxed his shoulders. Like he said earlier, it was nice to meet new folks. He smiled across the table at Ariana to let her know it was okay.

"What do you and Thomas do for a living?" Rennen asked, trying to draw the conversation away from him.

"I'm in the cosmetics business and Thomas in hospitality," Della said. She turned to Rennen, giving him a piercing look. "I was really touched by your interview."

So much for trying to deflect the attention from himself. "Thanks," he said offhandedly. He really didn't want to go into that tonight.

Della shook her head. "You have an interesting background." Her expression grew troubled. "I can't imagine what it must've been like to grow up like you did."

"Yeah, it was tough," Rennen admitted.

An uncomfortable silence descended on the table until Thomas spoke. "It sounds like it had a happy ending though. You found the one family."

Rennen knew Thomas was trying to lighten the mood. "Yes, the Boyds. They're like family to me."

Della shook her head, disgust heavy in her voice. "It's crazy how all those people are coming forward, claiming to be your parents." Compassion simmered in her eyes as she looked at him. "I'm sorry."

Rennen tightened his hold on his glass. "Thanks," he uttered. The air pressed around him, his heart thudding heavily in his chest. Now that his private life was on display for the world, he'd have to learn to come to terms with it. But it was hard. He looked at Ariana who was studying him intently. He could tell from the look on her face that she knew what he was feeling.

"What about you and Thomas?" Ariana asked. "How many children do you have?"

"Oh, Thomas and I aren't a couple," Della said. "We're just good friends."

This jolted Rennen out of his own head. Like Ariana, he'd assumed they were together. It just proved that you really couldn't tell what the true situation was with people until you got to know them.

"I have two sons," Thomas said. "One lives in Pittsburg and the other in upstate New York. My wife passed away a few years ago, and I've been on my own ever since."

"I'm sorry," Ariana said, as Thomas nodded.

All eyes turned to Della. Rennen was surprised to see tears gathering in her eyes. "I had one son." Her mouth started working. "I lost him when he was eighteen months old."

The grief on her face struck a chord with Rennen. Della had lost her son years ago, and yet, she was still suffering from the effect of it. Some hurts ran so deep that you could never really get over them.

"How did he die?" Ariana asked, her eyes radiating sympathy.

"I lost him because of cancer," Della squeaked. She brought a shaky hand to her mouth. "Sorry." She offered a strained smile. "It still gets to me ... sometimes, you know?"

"Yes, I know only too well," Rennen said softly.

Della looked at him and for a split second, he saw his own pain reflected in her eyes. A lump formed in his throat as he coughed to clear it. It was ironic. Both he and Della were suffering loss from the opposite sides of the coin. She'd lost her son. He'd lost his parents. The world could be so cruel sometimes.

Mindy returned with their food, which was a good thing or else they'd all be reduced to a miserable puddle of tears. They ate in companionable silence. Thomas was the first to speak. "Do you think you'll ever try to find out who your parents were?"

Rennen nearly choked on his steak. He took a swig of water to wash it down. He could feel Ariana's interest in the question, her eyes shooting lasers at him from across the table. "Probably not." He kept his voice light.

Della cocked her head. "Don't you want to know?"

It was scary how fast the anger surfaced. He clutched his napkin in his lap. "No, I don't. I have no interest in meeting the people who deserted their own flesh and blood."

"I can understand your anger," Della began, "but what if there's more to the story?"

This was sounding like an eerie repeat of the conversation

Rennen had with Ariana earlier. "In my experience, people will go to great lengths to craft a defense, try to rewrite history to help themselves sleep at night. But what possible defense can there be for a mother who deserts her child?" Rennen didn't try to hide the bitterness in his voice. "I needed my mother and father then, when I was hungry and alone, wandering around in a bus station. But I don't need them now." His voice shook with fury. He clenched his hands to stay the trembling. A shocked silence came over the table. "I'm sorry." He forced a smile. "You can tell I have strong feelings on the subject."

Ariana also smiled. "Rennen's been through a lot. We're working through it."

He gave her a look of appreciation, liking how she'd used the word *we*. "It's not all gloom and doom," he continued. "I was fortunate enough to find the Boyd family, who took me in as their own."

Della looked at Ariana. "And it looks like you've found a wonderful girl."

"Yes, I have." His eyes caressed Ariana's.

"And you have a wonderful career ahead of you," Thomas said. "You're really making a name for yourself in the football arena." He chuckled. "You and Ariana are making quite a splash with your relationship, considering the circumstances." He cleared his throat. "Um, with Ariana's brother."

Rennen tensed. Had Thomas really just said that? First, he and Della pushed their way into their dinner and now they were bringing up sensitive topics. He was about to put Thomas in his place when Ariana chuckled.

"Yeah, that's been interesting," she said, her eyes smiling at Rennen.

Rennen was surprised at Ariana's response. Maybe he was overreacting. He relaxed in his seat.

"I'd love to hear about it," Della said. "How did you and Rennen meet?"

Ariana smiled. "That's a very interesting story," she said as she proceeded to tell them the details.

Amusement sparked in Thomas's eyes. "Tell us about this rematch."

Rennen shook his head, chuckling. "Don't let Ariana fool you. She's little, but tough."

Ariana winked. "Better get ready for another butt-whooping, Goldie Locks."

Everyone laughed.

Della gave Ariana an appraising look. "I believe she's serious."

"Oh, absolutely," Rennen agreed. "She keeps me on my toes."

"It's seems like the two of you are very lucky to have each other," Della said. She placed her napkin on the table and leaned back in her seat. "Thanks so much for letting us join you tonight. It has been wonderful getting to know you."

"You're welcome," Rennen said, halfway meaning it. Della and Thomas seemed nice enough, but he didn't like being forced to talk about his past with strangers. There was that one moment, however, when he'd felt a strong connection to Della when she spoke of her child who'd passed.

Mindy returned and asked if they wanted dessert. They unanimously declined, declaring they were too full. "Here are your checks. I'll be your cashier when you're ready. Let me know if you need anything else."

Rennen reached for his check, but Thomas grabbed it first. "Allow me."

"I can't let you pay for our dinner," Rennen protested.

Della smiled smoothly. "It's the least we can do since we intruded on your evening."

"Thank you," Rennen said, feeling uncomfortable but grateful at the same time. At least Della had the good grace to acknowledge that she'd barged in on their dinner.

"If you're ever in Dallas/Ft. Worth, you should look us up," Ariana said. "My family owns a Mexican restaurant, Los Tios, and we'd love to have you."

Della smiled appreciatively. "Thank you. We should exchange numbers."

Ariana shrugged. "Sure."

After the checks were paid, Della and Thomas stood. "We'd better turn in for the night," Della said. "We've got a long day ahead of us tomorrow."

Rennen and Ariana also stood. Rennen was surprised when Della stepped over and gave him a tight hug. She looked into his eyes, her expression tender. "You're going to be all right ... despite everything."

Rennen was caught off guard by the emotion that rose in his throat as he nodded. "Thanks."

"Hopefully, we'll see each other again sometime," Thomas said, a smile stretching over his lips. "We'll have to give Los Tios a try."

As Della and Thomas walked away, Ariana stepped beside Rennen and slid an arm around his waist. "They seem nice."

He arched an eyebrow. "Yeah, for such an intrusive couple, they were moderately pleasant."

Ariana laughed. "They could've eased off on asking so many personal questions; but overall, I didn't think they were that bad."

He quirked a face. "Seriously? I felt like we were getting the third degree a few times."

A teasing grin slid over her lips. "If you think that was the third degree wait until you meet my mother."

He burst out laughing. "Should I be worried?"

"Petrified," she said straight-faced, then winked. "Nah, I'm sure you can hold your own." She cocked her head. "You know, it's strange, but Thomas looks so familiar to me."

"Really?"

"Yeah. But I can't place where I've seen him before." She shrugged. "He probably looks like someone who works out at the gym. That always happens to me. I'll meet someone in passing and then it'll bother me when I can't place the face."

Rennen pulled Ariana closer. "I'm glad they're gone," he murmured in her ear. "Because I get you all to myself."

She looked up at him, a large smile tipping her lips. "Do you wanna go back to our rooms, or do you wanna stay out here a little longer?"

Rennen was reluctant for the evening to end. "Let's go over and listen to the band for a while. Then maybe we can watch a movie in your room."

"Sounds like a plan to me."

As they walked arm in arm across the terrace, Rennen couldn't help but feel like he was the luckiest man in the world.

13

It had been a glorious evening. Rennen and Ariana spent a little over an hour listening to the band and even danced a couple of slow songs before making their way up to their rooms. Ariana suggested that they change into their pajamas before watching a movie. Rennen was pleased to see that Ariana kept the door to their adjoining rooms wide open.

He washed his face, then glanced at his reflection in the bathroom mirror as he dried off with a towel. He winced. He looked rough. His curls had turned to frizz in the humidity, making him look like he had a fro. He cupped his hands under the faucet and wet his hair. *Much better.* He reached in his travel bag for his toothbrush and toothpaste. He found the toothpaste, but no toothbrush. He searched through his bag. He'd used his toothbrush that morning at the Boyd's house. He frowned. Had he left his toothbrush in the Boyd's bathroom? Not wanting to go to the trouble of calling the front desk, he used his finger to brush his teeth. He swallowed a bit of toothpaste in the process, gagging.

When he stepped into Ariana's room, she was sitting on the bed, her back to him, talking on the phone.

Ariana sighed heavily, her tone laced with frustration. "Now's not the time to talk about this." Her voice rose. "I don't know when we can get together. I'll have to check my schedule and get back to you. I've gotta let you go, Paul."

Rennen's heart lurched. "Who's Paul?"

Ariana jerked around. "Hey." She laughed nervously.

Rennen's insecurities came flooding back with a vengeance as he shot Ariana an accusing look. "Who's Paul?" he repeated.

She placed her phone on the bedside table. "My ex."

Blood rushed to Rennen's temples. "Your ex-boyfriend?"

"Yeah. He's been trying to reach me for days, and I just now had a minute to call him back."

Rennen's throat went thick as he swallowed. "You keep in touch with your ex?"

She gave him a funny look. "Yeah. Paul and I were together for a long time. He's mostly just a friend."

He arched an eyebrow, his body tensing. "Mostly?"

Ariana's lips curved into a smile. "You're jealous." She stood and went to him, her eyes roving over his face. "Aren't you?"

"Do I have something to be jealous about?" He didn't like the idea of her toying with him.

"No, of course not." She slid her arms around his waist. "Don't get all bent out of shape. Everyone has a past. You probably have a long string of ex-girlfriends."

"Not that I keep in touch with," he shot back. Sure, he'd dated lots of girls, but none of them held a candle to Ariana. He'd never felt like this about anyone before. "Why was Paul calling you?" The jealousy stabbing him was so sharp it hurt his chest.

She let out a long breath. "Let's not go into this right now, okay?" Her voice took on an edge. "It's not important."

He put his arms around her, a fierce protectiveness overtaking him. He couldn't stand the thought of Ariana ever being with anyone else. He searched her face, craving reassurance that all was well between them.

She lifted her face to his, her hands going up to cup his cheeks. "Paul is my past. You're my future. I love you."

"I love you too," he said, a silly grin washing over his face. It had been stupid to get so worked up about Ariana's ex. Ariana was here with him, not Paul. Her beauty, the essence of her wafted over him as he pulled her closer, drinking in her scent. His lips captured hers, and he kissed her like he'd wanted to all evening, holding nothing back.

14

The next week seemed to fly by with Ariana and Rennen spending every moment they could together, which wasn't as much as they would've liked considering Rennen's daily training sessions and her hectic work schedule. Ariana knew it was only a matter of time before she'd have to introduce Rennen to her family, but she wanted to keep him to herself a little longer first.

Maybe she'd wait until after the rematch was over tomorrow. After that, she and Rennen could settle into their lives ... *somewhat.* Ariana knew from Ace's experience that as soon as the football season got underway, Rennen would be going nonstop. Ariana was getting used to the throng of reporters that had taken up residence outside her gym. They peppered her with questions as she came and went. She'd always look straight ahead and utter, "no comment," dismissing them from her mind like pesky flies. Ariana hoped they would lose interest after the rematch. Her mind flitted to the two-hundred grand. She wondered if she'd have enough to add saunas in the dressing rooms. That would be nice.

"Whatever daydream you're having ... I want in."

She jumped, turning to Beth. "What?"

"Judging by the ginormous grin on your face, you've got to be thinking about Rennen."

She laughed. "Is it that obvious?"

"You're in love," Beth cooed. "And I have to admit, you did score a great one."

"Yeah, I kind of did, didn't I?" A burst of happiness enveloped her. She'd never imagined love could be this amazing. There was a time when Ariana had thought she might be in love with Paul. But in comparison to the real deal, she realized that she only cared about Paul as a good friend. Too bad he didn't feel the same way. Paul had been calling her nonstop, begging her to get together with him so they could talk. She kept putting him off but would eventually have to put closure on the situation. She and Paul had left it that they were dating other people but would still see each other occasionally. She'd have to break it to him that she was no longer on the market. Of course, Paul must realize that after seeing the media frenzy over her and Rennen. Her phone rang. She reached for it, not recognizing the number.

"Hello?"

"Hello. This is Della Chastain. We met at The Hideaway Inn."

"Hi, Della." Ariana couldn't imagine why she would be calling. Sure they'd exchanged numbers, but it was more of a formality. Something you did out of decorum, never expecting to hear from the person again.

"You're probably wondering why I'm calling."

"Yes."

Long pause.

For a second, Ariana thought they'd lost the connection. "Della? Are you there?"

"Yes."

That's when Ariana noticed that Della's voice sounded strange, too high-pitched. "Are you okay?"

"Is there any way we could meet for lunch?"

Ariana scrambled to keep up. "Are you in Ft. Worth?"

"Yes, Thomas and I are headed back to New York. But we thought we'd stop by here first."

"Okay." That was odd. "When would you like to have lunch? Or dinner maybe? I can check with Rennen to see if we can make something work."

"I was kind of hoping we could get together today."

Ariana's eyes widened. "Today?"

"Yes, if that's okay."

She shook her head. "I'm sorry, I need more notice."

"Please. There's something important I need to talk to you about."

This conversation was getting weirder by the minute. Della had seemed perfectly normal, but maybe she wasn't. Maybe their meeting at the inn wasn't a coincidence. "Yeah, sorry, it's not gonna work. Like I said, I've got a lot going on today." Something about this situation was off.

"I can come to you."

She was starting to get a little freaked out. "No, that's not a good idea."

"It's about Rennen," Della blurted. "Something I need to tell you."

Ariana tightened her hold on the phone. What was Della playing at? "If it's something important, then maybe you should tell me now."

"I'll meet you at Café Pierpont, just around the corner from your gym in twenty minutes. Please, it's very important."

Before Ariana could respond, Della ended the call.

Beth gave her a funny look. "What was that about? Are you okay?"

Ariana shook her head. "I'm not sure. Rennen and I met this couple at the inn where we stayed, and now the woman—Della—is wanting to have lunch."

"Seems harmless enough."

"Yeah, I suppose. But Della and her friend Thomas don't live here. They're from New York. She says she has something important to tell me about Rennen." Her heart thudded against her ribcage.

Beth's eyes registered surprise. "That's strange."

"Yeah, very."

"Are you gonna meet her?"

It then occurred to Ariana that Della somehow knew that she owned a gym and the location of it. They hadn't talked about that, had they?

"Maybe you should call Rennen and get his take on it," Beth said.

Ariana nodded. "Good idea."

She called him, her heart dropping when it went to voicemail. "Hey, it's me. Call me when you can." She shook her head. "Rennen's tied up all day. He had training this morning. His agent flew in today and they're meeting at the PR firm to make sure everything's set for the rematch."

Beth's features tightened. "Do you think this woman's a threat? Maybe you should call the police."

Ariana laughed in surprise. "No, I don't think she's a threat. She seems like a classy lady."

Beth shrugged. "Then maybe you should meet her ... hear what she has to say."

"Yeah, maybe." Ariana's curiosity was piqued. What could Della possibly have to tell her about Rennen? Café Pierpont was a safe enough location, lots of people coming and going. If Ariana didn't meet Della she'd probably show up here at the gym. It was better to meet her at a neutral place. "Okay, I'll go. But if I'm not back in an hour, then you'll know something's wrong."

"Should I call Tina to watch the front desk and come with you?" Beth asked, concern etching her features.

Ariana waved a hand. "No, that's okay. I'm sure it'll be fine." She slung her purse over her shoulder. "Wish me luck."

CAFÉ PIERPONT WAS KNOWN for being busy at lunch and today was no exception. Ariana tried calling Rennen on the drive over, but couldn't reach him. She drew in a calming breath as she turned off her truck engine and got out. As she stepped into the café, she spotted Della sitting at a booth in the back corner. When Della saw her, she smiled. "Thanks for coming," she said, as Ariana slid into the seat.

Ariana drew her lips together nodding. It was shocking to see the transformation in Della since she'd last seen her. The lines around her mouth and eyes were more pronounced. Dark circles were carved under her eyes, making her glasses look like they had extra rings around them. And she had a hollow look, like she'd not slept in days.

"Did Thomas not come with you?"

Della cut her eyes at the table across the room where Thomas was sitting alone. He was holding a menu, his eyes peering over it as he watched them. A jolt went through Ariana as she remembered why Thomas looked familiar. He was the silver-haired man watching her and Rennen at The Red Table on the night of their first date. She tightened her fist, glaring at Della. "Are you a reporter?" Disappointment rankled her gut. She'd thought Della and Thomas were such nice people, but they'd been playing them the entire time.

"No, I'm not a reporter." Della's voice was weary.

Ariana tried to piece it all together. "Why is Thomas sitting over there?"

"He wanted to give us a chance to talk alone."

Ariana sat back, folding her hands tightly over her chest as she leveled a glare at Della. "Why did you want to see me?"

Della let out a long sigh and reached for her glass. Her hand shook as she took a drink of water and set the glass back down. "My real name is Delphine Degarmo." She spoke the words like they were supposed to mean something. When Ariana shook her head dubiously, Delphine continued. "I own Bella Bisou cosmetics."

Her breath hitched. Now that meant something. Bella Bisou was one of the largest cosmetic companies in the world. Of course Ariana recognized that. Every girl who wore makeup would. "Beautiful Kiss," she uttered, repeating the American translation of the French phrase.

Delphine nodded. "Yes."

Ariana felt like she was in a sparring match with an opponent who switched positions so quickly she could hardly stay with her, much less pin her down. She looked across the table, repeating all she knew to find some thread that would help her understand what was going on. "Your real name's not Della Chastain, but Delphine

Degarmo." Now that she thought about it, the name did sound familiar aside from the cosmetic line. Where had she heard it before? She searched her mind. "Aren't you some French heiress? A socialite turned businesswoman?" She could tell from the look on Delphine's face that she was on the right track.

"My father's name was Renatus." She waved a hand. "A well-known family in France. My father was the sole heir to the Renatus fortune."

"What does your father or his fortune have to do with this?"

Delphine reached in her purse and pulled out a photo. She slid it across the table to Ariana who picked it up and gasped. The man in the picture bore a startling resemblance to Rennen. It all came together in a hard jolt. Ariana sat there, stunned. Then her eyes narrowed as she gave Delphine a hard look. "You're Rennen's mother."

"Yes."

Ariana's mind whirled, bringing a wave of nausea. "Why would a woman like you abandon her own son? And why are you here talking to me instead of Rennen?"

A pained smile stretched over Delphine's lips. "I had no idea Rennen was my son. I'd given up hope of ever finding him until I saw the Katie Moss interview."

"And saw how much he looks like your father," Ariana supplied.

"I still wasn't sure ... even then." Her hand went up to smooth her hair. "The only way I could be positive was to do a DNA test."

Ariana's brows furrowed. "Is that why you followed us to the inn?" She felt so used. Betrayed. Hot prickles covered her. Rennen was not going to take this well. They'd sat together at dinner, talked about personal things. And all the while, Rennen's mother had been right beside him. To make matters worse, thanks to this little meeting at the café, Ariana was now right in the middle of it. Heat blazed up her neck. "I can't believe you were right there with us and didn't say a word."

She spread her hands. "I couldn't say anything, not until I knew for sure. You can imagine how terrible that would've been for Rennen if I'd claimed to be his mother, then found out I really wasn't." She shuddered. "He's been through enough already."

"Yes, he has," Ariana shot through clenched teeth. "Because of you." Her mind went back to something Delphine said. "Were you gathering DNA evidence at the inn? Is that why you pushed your way into our dinner?"

Tears pooled in her eyes as she touched her glasses. "No, I just wanted to be able to talk to my son."

"What kind of evidence did you gather?"

"A toothbrush ... hair."

"You broke into Rennen's room and stole those things?"

"Yes." She hesitated. "I know how this sounds, and I understand why you're upset."

"Oh, I'm more than upset." Ariana leaned forward, her eyes burning. "I'm fighting mad. And what you're seeing now is nothing compared to what you'll get when Rennen hears about this."

Delphine nodded. "That's why I'm here. I hoped to be able to tell Rennen all this myself." She hesitated. "Unfortunately, the story will break before I get the chance."

Alarm trickled over Ariana. "What do you mean?"

"I tried to be discreet about the DNA test, but someone leaked the information. I found out this morning from a trusted source that the story will air in the next twenty-four hours."

Ariana's eyes bulged as she clutched her neck. "You've got to stop it!"

Delphine shook her head. "I tried." She let out a brittle laugh. "Believe me, I tried." A sour expression twisted her face. "Unfortunately, anything surrounding the Bella Bisou empire is big news. Plus the fact that Rennen is now a celebrity. There's no stopping this."

Ariana's nails dug into her palms as she balled her fists. "Rennen's not going to take this well at all."

"I know." Delphine's mouth vanished into a thin line.

"Why did you want to meet with me? Why not tell Rennen this yourself?"

"I didn't have his number."

Ariana arched an eyebrow. "I'm not buying that. A woman of your influence could've found a way to get in touch with him."

Delphine fingered her napkin. "That night at dinner, when I realized how bitter Rennen was ..." her voice broke "... I was afraid." She gave Ariana a hopeful look. "But he'll listen to you. I can tell the two of you are close. You help round off his hard edges."

A disbelieving laugh broke from Ariana's throat. "Seriously? This is between you and Rennen. I have nothing to do with it." She shot Delphine a blistering look. "And frankly, like Rennen said, what possible excuse could you have for abandoning your own child?" She shook her head, disgust heavy in her voice. "You sat there and told us all that stuff about how your son had died of cancer. None of that was true, was it? Was it?" she repeated, her voice escalating.

Delphine's face drained. "I said I had lost my son because of cancer. You assumed that meant he died, so I left it at that."

"No, you led us to believe that was the case." Ariana's voice was hard as flint. There was no way she was letting Delphine weasel out of this. What did that even mean anyway—*lost her son because of cancer?*

"Much of what I told you was true."

"Much?" she flung back. "Sorry, that doesn't cut it."

"If you'll just hear me out, you'll understand how it happened." Desperation coated her voice. "Please."

The server approached the table in a huff as she retrieved her pad from her apron. "I'm so sorry it took me a while to get over here. This place is a madhouse today." She looked at Ariana. "What can I get you to drink?"

"A Dr. Pepper ... the biggest one you've got," Ariana muttered.

The server tried to take their food orders, but both Delphine and Ariana declined, saying they'd just stick with their drinks. After the girl left, Ariana sat back in her seat, eyeing Delphine. "Okay, I'm all ears."

15

Rennen, Monroe, and Lainey sat around the conference room table at the DaVinci PR firm. It had been a hectic morning. Training ran over a full hour, then Rennen had to hurry and get showered so he could meet Monroe and Lainey for this brainstorm session. Unfortunately, a swarm of reporters cornered him as he exited the Titan Training Complex to get to his car, pummeling him with questions about his and Ariana's relationship. It astounded Rennen that people were so consumed with everything he was doing.

Monroe and Lainey sat across from Rennen, heads close together, having an in-depth conversation about Rennen's talking points for the reporters. Rennen knew he should be more involved in the process, but he was having a hard time concentrating. His mind ran through the quick phone conversation he'd had with Ariana before darting into this meeting. She'd asked if he could meet her somewhere to talk. Unfortunately, that wasn't possible. He'd be tied up at this meeting and having dinner with Monroe afterwards. Ariana's voice was tense ... worried. He could tell something was wrong. A part of him wondered if he should bag dinner and find out what was going on.

No, he had to stick with the plan. Monroe had flown in to meet with him. It wouldn't be fair to leave him in the lurch. He promised Ariana that he'd stop by her house tonight, as soon as dinner was over. He asked her to just tell him what was wrong over the phone, but she insisted that they needed to talk in person. A knot formed in his stomach. Was she having second thoughts about the two of them? Everything had been going so well. As soon as the rematch was over, Ariana planned to introduce Rennen to her family. Sweat broke across his forehead as he went hot all over. His heart began to pound.

"Hey, man, are you okay? You look a little flushed."

Rennen forced a smile. "I'm all right. Just starting to feel a bit of the pressure."

Monroe nodded in understanding. "I hear ya. Unfortunately, it's about to get worse before it gets better. The press has been sharpening their knives, howling that this whole rematch is a big publicity stunt."

"Well, of course it's a publicity stunt," Rennen grumbled. "Everyone knows the fight between me and Ariana is for fun."

"Now that you and Ariana are official, it puts a different spin on things," Lainey added, reproof ringing in her voice.

Rennen's head began to spin, dread clutching his heart like a vise. Something was wrong. Terribly wrong. He couldn't wait until tonight to talk to Ariana. He had to talk to her now. He scooted back his chair, giving Monroe an apologetic look. "I'm sorry, but I need to cut this meeting short. There's something I have to—"

A woman ran into the room, a shocked expression on her face. "Turn on the TV," she ordered. "There's something you need to see."

Lainey peered over her glasses. "Susan, what's going on? You know I don't approve of you interrupting my meetings in this fashion."

Susan wrung her hands. "I'm sorry, Mrs. Summerfield. But you'll wanna see this. Trust me."

Lainey frowned as she reached for the remote in the center of the table and turned on the TV.

At first, Rennen couldn't make sense of what he was seeing and hearing.

Monroe swore loudly, pounding the table with his fist. He spun around to Lainey. "How could you let this happen? This is why Rennen hired you. To prevent crap like this."

She rocked back, her face going rigid. "This is not my fault." She looked at Rennen, daggers shooting from her eyes. "I warned you that something like this could happen. Tried to meet with you to come up with a plan to contain it, but you wouldn't listen."

Her accusations came at Rennen from a distance. All he could hear was the roaring in his own ears as he looked at the screen, trying to comprehend all that was happening. He forced himself to concentrate on the news report being delivered by a peppy reporter with an enthusiastic smile stretched over her face.

"DNA tests confirm that Delphine Degarmo, French heiress and owner of Bella Bisou cosmetics is, in fact, the birth mother of Texas Titan running back Rennen Bradley."

A picture flashed on the screen. Rennen gulped in a ragged breath, recognizing the woman instantly—Della, from the inn. He clutched the arms of the chair.

Monroe shot him a worried look. "You don't look so good, man."

Invisible fingers clutched Rennen's throat as he fought to get a good breath.

"Wait, there's more," the reporter said. Another picture flashed on the screen. Rennen's eyes bulged. "This photo of Delphine Degarmo and Ariana Sanchez was taken a couple of hours ago at Café Pierpont in Ft. Worth. You'll remember that Ariana Sanchez is the sister of Ace Sanchez. Rennen took Ace's spot on the Titans. He and Ariana Sanchez have been spotted together several times."

"Well isn't this just peachy?" Lainey said, throwing up her hands. She turned to Monroe. "Now what?"

The reporter continued, laying out all the details of Rennen's life in cold, hard facts. A bitter hurt sliced through him sending tremors over his body. Why had Ariana met with Della Chastain behind his back? Is that what Ariana had wanted to talk to him about? How long had Ariana known that Della was his mother? Della had sat right beside him at dinner, spoke of her son who died of cancer. Was anything she said even true? Somehow he doubted it. His mind was on fire. It was bad enough to be abandoned at a bus station by some poor, downtrodden mother. But a billionaire heiress? The owner of a worldwide cosmetic company? And to think that Ariana was somehow mixed up in this. He stumbled to his feet.

"Hey, man," Monroe said. "You need to take it easy. Let all of this settle in."

Rage boiled through him as he bolted for the door. He had to get to Ariana and find out what in the heck was going on.

ARIANA PACED BACK and forth across her living room—four steps forward, four steps back. After her conversation with Delphine, she'd gone back to the gym and tried to get some work done, but was too keyed up to concentrate. Finally, she'd called a sub to teach her last two classes and came home. Now that she was here, she wished she'd stayed at the gym. At least there she had something to occupy her mind. Here, she was just worrying herself sick.

Delphine said news of the DNA test would break in less than twenty-four hours. Meaning, she still had plenty of time to tell Rennen the news ... *hopefully.* Maybe Ariana should've just told Rennen everything over the phone. No, it would come as too big of a shock to him. Heck, it was a shock to Ariana and it wasn't even her past. She had to tell Rennen in person. Of all the days for something like this to happen, the one day when Rennen was tied up with his agent.

A knock sounded at the door. She rushed to answer it, thinking it might be Ace. She'd asked him to come over, needing a sounding board to help her figure out how to break the news of Della to Rennen. Or maybe Rennen changed his mind and decided to come over early. She threw open the door. Her shoulders fell when she saw who it was. "Paul."

A tentative smile spread over his face as he held out a bouquet of flowers.

A hysterical laugh gurgled in her throat. "You're bringing me flowers?" His timing couldn't have been lousier.

Reflexively, she reached for the flowers, not bothering to bring them to her nose. "Thanks," she said flatly, letting her arm fall by her side, the heads of the flowers nearly touching the floor.

He searched her face. "I've missed you."

She tried to think of a way to let him down gently. "I'm sorry, Paul. You're a great guy ... and a good friend," she began.

His eyes took on a wounded look. "It's because of Rennen Bradley, isn't it?"

"Yes." She forced a smile. "I'm sorry. You don't plan on these things. They just happen."

"I thought you hated football players."

"So did I," she countered with a dry chuckle.

He motioned. "Can I at least come in?"

She planted her feet, blocking the entrance. "I don't think that's a good idea."

An awkward silence froze between them.

Finally, Paul nodded. "For what it's worth I really do love you."

She didn't know how to answer.

He leaned forward and gave her a peck on the mouth. "Goodbye," he uttered.

"Well, this is interesting."

Ariana flinched, pulling back from Paul, her eyes bulging. "Rennen," she gulped, a hot embarrassment stinging her cheeks as she thought about how this must look. Her holding flowers, Paul kissing her lips.

A furious expression twisted over Rennen as he balled his fists. His body was taut, a panther, ready to pounce. Then he shot Ariana a withering look that cut her to the quick. "How could you?" he uttered.

Confusion swirled over her. "This is not what it looks like. Paul was just coming to say goodbye." Rennen's face turned a deep purple, and he looked like he was going to blow—a bull shuffling his feet in the dust, looking for the red flag so he could charge.

Rennen let out a harsh laugh. "It looked like he was doing a lot more than that."

Paul turned to Ariana with a grunt. "Is this really the guy you're dumping me for? Some knucklehead?"

The condescension in Paul's voice tromped on her last nerve. She was about to put him in his place when everything imploded. Ariana saw it in slow motion—the savage look in Rennen's eyes the instant before he hauled off and socked Paul, knocking him to the ground.

"What're you doing?" Ariana yelled, dropping the flowers.

Paul's eyes bulged with fear as he held his nose, which was gushing blood. "I think he broke my nose," he wailed.

Rennen hovered over him. "I'll break a lot more than that. Get up," he thundered.

Paul ducked into himself as he averted his eyes.

Ariana reached for Rennen's arm, spinning him around. "What's wrong with you?" she yelled, a swift anger overtaking her.

"How could you?" Rennen growled, getting in her face.

"How could I what?"

His voice caught as he gurgled. "Meet with Della behind my back."

Her heart dropped. "H—how did you know?"

A crazed look came into Rennen's eyes as he thundered. "The whole world knows! It's all over the news."

She swallowed, a deep weariness settling over her. "That's why I wanted to talk to you. I only found out today." Before she could tell him the rest, he cut her off.

"I trusted you," he seethed. "Believed you loved me." He shot Paul a blistering look. "Not only did you go behind my back with my mother, but with him as well!"

Ariana couldn't believe what she was hearing. The sting of his words came at her like a swarm of angry bees. "I told you, I only found out about your mother today. And Paul was coming to say goodbye. I told him it was over. Furthermore, if you'll just shut up a minute and listen, you might have a different opinion of your mother."

"I don't want a different opinion," he roared.

"If you'll just listen to me."

"Save it," he sneered. "I can't trust you or anyone else." He shook his head. "I should've known you were too good to be true."

The coldness in his eyes froze her heart. Somehow, she managed to find her voice. "That's right. It's you against the world, isn't it Rennen? You've spent your whole life holding onto your anger like it's some prize. Waiting for the world to disappoint you."

He clenched his jaw, pointing at his chest, his voice going ragged. "My struggles made me who I am. I won't let you or anyone else get in my head."

"You keep standing up there on your tower, judging the world." Her voice broke as she swallowed back the tears. She'd be darned if she let him see her cry. "Well, I've got news for you, buddy, the only person impeding your happiness is you." Tears brimmed in her eyes. "You expect everyone around you to let you down, and it becomes a self-fulfilling prophecy. I can't be in a relationship with someone who's always waiting for me to fail." She turned to Paul, venting her anger on him. "Get your butt up," she ordered. "Let's get you inside and get you cleaned up."

Paul rose to his feet, glaring at Rennen. "You'll be hearing from my attorney."

Ariana barked out a laugh. "Oh, shut up, Paul. You are an attorney. This stops here and now. You won't sue Rennen, not if you value our friendship."

When Rennen smirked out a justified laugh, she spun at him. "I pity you. All the happiness in the world at your feet and you're too stupid to recognize it."

Rennen looked at her for a long moment. She thought she caught a blip of something in his eyes that made her hope she might be getting through to him. But then a curtain came over his face as he turned and stalked away, breaking her heart into a million unrecognizable pieces.

16

Rennen's mind was a blur as he got in his car and jabbed the key into the ignition. His phone buzzed. It was Monroe. He was tempted to let it go to voicemail but knew Monroe would keep calling until he answered. "Hello," he barked.

"Hey, man. Where'd you go?"

"Out!" The poisonous fog infesting his brain made it hard to form a clear thought. Ariana accused him of holding his anger like a prize, waiting for everyone to fail him. Was that what he was doing? He replayed the wounded look in her eyes when he told her she was too good to be true. It was a stupid thing to say. He gripped the steering wheel. When he saw Ariana at her door, Paul kissing her, he'd lost all reason. And then she told him she couldn't be in a relationship with someone who kept expecting her to fail. A trickle of fear ran down his spine. Surely she wasn't saying it was over between them. They'd had one lousy fight, that was all. Maybe he should go back in right now, apologize. He'd obviously misread the situation between Ariana and Paul.

But this thing with his mother ... he didn't know how in the heck to come to terms with it. It was so incredible ... ridiculous that his mother was a billionaire heiress. She'd had the audacity to sit beside him at dinner while he spilled his guts about his past. What possible excuse could Delphine have for abandoning him? The old familiar hurt slithered around his chest like an anaconda, cutting off his breath. No one understood the depth of the pain he'd endured.

"Rennen, are you there?"

He realized Monroe was still on the phone. "Uh, yeah," he croaked. He needed to get a grip. He gulped in a breath. *In through the mouth ... out through the nose.* He had to be strong, couldn't let this get to him.

"You need to get back here to the DaVinici Firm ASAP."

He rubbed a hand across his forehead. "I know we planned on going to dinner tonight, but under the circumstance, maybe we should cancel." His voice dribbled off.

"This isn't about dinner. This is about Delphine Degarmo. More information has surfaced. Things you'll be interested to hear."

A scorching anger seared through him, clouding out all reason. "I don't want to hear anything else about that woman," he yelled. His wretched mother had already caused him enough pain to last a lifetime. He just wanted it to stop.

Monroe's voice rose to match his volume. "Trust me. You'll wanna hear this, man. You need to get back here. Right now!"

He blew out a long breath. "Fine," he grumbled. "But there's something I need to take care of first." He was going back this instant to resolve things with Ariana. He couldn't stand the thought of her being mad at him, and he couldn't stand the thought of her being in her apartment alone with Paul. They'd both said things ... stupid things they couldn't leave dangling.

"Rennen, I can't think of anything in this world that's more important to you than getting your butt back over here on the double. This can't wait. I'm begging you, man. You need to come now!"

The urgency in Monroe's voice pricked him, cutting through the fog for an instant. He had to face this thing with his mother. That was the only way he'd be free of it. Rennen glanced at Ariana's apartment complex. "All right," he finally said, starting his engine. "I'm on my way."

"YOU'D BETTER HAVE a good explanation for dragging me back over here," Rennen said as he stormed into the conference room, then stopped dead in his tracks when he saw who was sitting at the table with Monroe and Lainey. His eyes narrowed as he looked at Delphine. "What're you doing here?" Fury zigzagged through him like a thousand knives gutting his insides as he held up his hands. "I'm not doing this."

Monroe jumped to his feet. "You need to hear her out."

Rennen's pulse roared like a jet engine through his ears as he shook his head. "No!" He shot Monroe a venomous look. "I told you I didn't want to talk to her. Not now or ever!"

Monroe shook his head, a frustrated laugh gurgling in his throat. "It's not what you think, man. If you'll just sit down and listen—"

Delphine stood. "Rennen, sit down." Her voice was surprisingly calm, but it pierced Rennen to the core. Her eyes locked with his. "If you don't like what I have to say, then you never have to see me again. But at least you'll hear the truth from me, not from those dastardly reporters who make their livings off the misery of others."

The air seemed to hold its breath as Rennen contemplated what he would do. Finally, he strode over to a chair and sat down. The feeling of despondency that settled over Rennen was so strong he could taste it. It oozed from the walls and dripped down the floors, pouring around his feet where it pumped poison into his veins. Nothing this woman could say would change anything, but he'd at least hear her out.

Delphine and Monroe took their seats. Delphine adjusted her blouse, then touched her glasses, clearing her throat. She took in a deep breath, offering Rennen a faint smile. "This is harder than I thought it would be."

Rennen just sat there, stone-faced. It was still hard to believe his flesh and blood mother was sitting across the table. Looking at her now he could see the resemblance. Similar hair color, similar bone structure. He'd often pictured how his mother would look. Deep down, he'd always figured his mother was probably an unwed teenager or druggie who couldn't handle the responsibility of having a child. Never, in a million years, would he have imagined his mother being a wealthy French heiress.

"I'm not sure what you've heard from the news," Delphine said.

"Only that DNA tests confirm that you're my biological mother." Rennen didn't try to hide the resentment in his voice.

Delphine wet her lips, nodding. "I'll just tell you everything, from the beginning. That way, you'll get the whole picture. As you know, my real name is Delphine Degarmo. My father's name was Renatus." A faint smile touched her lips as she looked at Rennen. "You were named after my father."

Rennen sat rigged, clutching his hands. He felt like all of this was happening to someone else.

"My mother died when I was born, and I was raised by my father who had no idea how to take care of a daughter, other than to send me off to a boarding school." She laughed regretfully. "As you can imagine, I was spoiled and impetuous. My father tried to groom me to take over his inheritance, but I was determined to live my life on my own terms, by my own rules. When I was in my early twenties, I had an affair with a married man and got pregnant with you."

Rennen let out a harsh laugh. "So I was an embarrassment that you wanted to get rid of? Is that why you abandoned me?"

"No, you were never an embarrassment to me." Tears gathered in her eyes. "I loved you with all my heart." Her voice caught as she touched her neck and cleared her throat. She gave him a strained smile. "You were a blessing straight from heaven."

Confusion swirled in Rennen. "Then why?" The words got lodged in his throat as he tried again. "Why did you abandon me?"

Delphine looked him in the eye. "I didn't abandon you."

Rennen's heart skipped a beat. "What? I don't understand."

She chuckled, remembering. "When I had you, I knew I had to change. I had to become better ... become the mother you deserved." She lifted her chin. "So I did. I put aside my reckless ways." She paused, pain coloring her features. "I remember the day like it was yesterday." Her voice grew strangled. "October 28, 1992, a beautiful, crisp, fall day. You were eighteen months old. I took you to Central Park. You were playing on the playground, and I was watching you from a nearby bench. It was crowded with other children and families." Her voice took on an odd note. "I was distracted. I had just learned a few hours earlier that I had stage-three breast cancer." Her lower lip trembled. "I took my eyes off you for one minute, and you were gone. Just like that." Tears rolled down Delphine's cheeks. She lifted her glasses and wiped at them. Lainey handed her a tissue.

Rennen grunted in surprise. A buzz ran through his head as he knotted his fists. "You're telling me I was kidnapped?"

"Yes. I searched the park from top to bottom, going out of my mind. The police were called, people at the park questioned. But no one saw anything suspicious." Her voice broke. "I hold myself responsible. I should've never taken you to the park, not in that frame of mind."

Rennen tried to sift through what he was hearing. "But money was no object for you. How could you not find me?"

"Things were different in 1992. The Internet wasn't mainstream. Legal agencies didn't report to each other the way they do now. No Amber Alerts." Her voice sounded old and haggard. "When the police didn't turn up any leads, I hired a team of investigators." She squared her jaw. "I was determined to do everything in my power to find you."

He'd not been abandoned, but kidnapped? He looked across the table at Delphine. He'd had a mother who loved him, had mourned his absence. All his life he'd gotten it totally wrong, been seeing the world through a defective pair of lenses. A gush of emotion rose in his throat, sending tears to his eyes. The foundation of everything he'd ever believed was crumbling before his very eyes, and he wasn't sure what to feel. Anger? Sorrow? It was all mixed in a bundle of fire that felt like lead in the center of his chest. "How did I end up in Texas?"

Delphine shrugged. "I don't know." Her face hardened. "I assume someone kidnapped you with the intent to sell you. But who knows?"

A furrow appeared between Rennen's brows. "If news of my kidnapping was so far spread, you'd think someone would've recognized me."

Monroe tilted his head, looking thoughtful. "Not necessarily. You said the first memory you have is of being in a group home, right?"

Rennen nodded.

"And before that, you were in another foster home. But were taken away because it was suspected that you were being abused."

"That's right." Rennen wasn't making the connection.

Monroe looked at him. "How long were you in that first foster situation?"

"About a year, from what I was told. Although I don't have any memory of it."

"So your first real memory was when you were what? Six or seven?"

Rennen thought back. "Yes."

"You were kidnapped when you were eighteen months old," Monroe continued, "which leaves a gap of roughly three and a half years. Someone could've kept you hidden for that amount of time and then dumped you at the bus station."

"Yeah, I guess anything's possible." Rennen felt the all-too-familiar frustration bubble inside him. It was so dang infuriating not to have any knowledge of what happened to him.

Anger flashed in Delphine's eyes. "I have another theory."

All eyes turned to her.

"I was fighting for my life, going through chemotherapy and radiation—so weak I could barely lift my head." Her voice shook. "I had no other choice but to let my father spearhead the search for you." Her mouth twisted. "I fought cancer for three long years, thinking everything possible was being done to find you. The first few hours are critical in a kidnapping case, and then come the first few days, months, and years. As more time passes, the trail goes cold. I didn't find out until ten years later that my father hadn't done everything in his power to find you. It wasn't until my father was on his deathbed that he told me the truth. He was relieved you were taken. Relieved that I wouldn't be burdened with raising a child on my own, like he'd been. Relieved that the family name wouldn't be tainted any longer by an illegitimate child." A sob wrenched her throat. She put a hand to her mouth, her shoulders shaking. She took in a ragged breath, trying to gain control of her emotions.

Delphine removed her glasses, placing them on the table, then looked at Rennen with pleading eyes. "A part of me died the day I lost you. For years, I prayed every day that I would find you. As time went on, I began to lose hope. My prayers changed. I prayed that if the Lord wouldn't allow me to find you, that He'd lead you to a good family." She smiled through her tears. "That portion of my prayer was answered. He sent the Boyds to you. I will forever be grateful to them."

Rennen gulped, trying to cough back the emotion, but it came shooting up like a geyser as a groan escaped his throat. He gulped, tears rolling down his cheeks.

"You need to know that I've never stopped trying to find you. I hired investigator after investigator." She let out a harsh laugh. "Of course I never dreamt that you were in Texas. I had no idea where you were, or even if you were still alive. But still I clung to the hope that I would someday see you again." A weak smile touched her lips. "You can imagine my surprise when Thomas, my long-time chauffeur and friend, showed me your interview with Katie Moss. I sat there, unable to believe my eyes." She laughed to herself. "All these years of searching, and there you were—plain as day."

Rennen wiped at his tears with the palms of his hands. "How did you know it was me?"

"Because you look so much like my father." She looked at Lainey who slid a picture across the table to Rennen. He gasped when he saw it. Same hair, same eyes, same determined set of the chin. Resentment surged through his veins. His grandfather hadn't wanted him, had considered him an embarrassment. If he'd really searched for him, then all of this could've been avoided. He realized Delphine was speaking.

"Like I said, you were named after my father Renatus. I called you

René." Her eyes cut into his. "But as a child, you couldn't pronounce it."

His eyes bulged as he connected the dots. "It sounded like Rennen," he gurgled. He shook his head. "I always thought I was given that name by a social worker." His head was spiraling like a renegade football. "Why didn't you tell me this when you saw me at the inn?"

"I didn't know for sure. I didn't want to tell you and be wrong. I had to collect DNA evidence. Your toothbrush and hair."

He balled his fists to stay the trembling in his hands. His throat grew thick as he swallowed, looking across the table at his mother. He'd longed for this day, prayed for it continually in his youth. And then his heart had turned to stone as he picked himself up and got on with his life.

She smiled through her tears. "You and I are more alike than you realize. When I overcame the cancer, I put my energy into searching for you. I was like some demented fool, determined to find you." Her voice sounded heavy and labored. "But by that time, too many years had passed. I reached a point, where I knew if I didn't channel my energy elsewhere, I'd go crazy. I kept a team of investigators on retainer, then turned my sights to building my cosmetic business." She smiled thinly. "My work became my obsession."

"Just as football became mine," Rennen added quietly.

Delphine eyed Rennen with such intensity that he felt like she was seeing into his soul. "Finding you has been a dream come true." Her voice quivered. "I want to be part of your life. But when I realized how angry and bitter you were ..." She paused. "I panicked and called Ariana, hoping she could talk to you first ... to pave the way for me. Then the story broke sooner than I expected." She shrugged, giving him a tiny smile. "Now you know the full story. What you choose to do with it is up to you." Her voice quivered. "Hate me if you must. But know this. I love you, son. I've always loved you and will never stop."

Tears filled Rennen's eyes as a dam broke loose inside him. He laughed through the tears. Something Ariana said came rushing back. All the happiness in the world was at his feet, if only he wasn't too stupid to take hold of it. Before he realized what he was doing, he was on his feet and rushing around the table. Delphine got to her feet as he crushed her in a hug.

He buried his face in Delphine's hair, inhaling her scent. A sense of something long-ago forgotten and tenuously familiar washed over him as a single word wrenched his throat. "Mom."

"I'm so glad I found you," she breathed. "You're a ghost no longer."

17

The Titan practice field was buzzing with so many reporters and other seemingly important people that Ariana hardly recognized it as the place where she and Rennen had initially sparred. A boxing ring was set up in the center of the field with bleachers extending out on all four sides like endless ripples from a rock thrown in a pond. From what Ariana could tell, every inch of the bleachers was filled. Ariana was standing inside the ring, waiting for Rennen to arrive. She glanced up at the Jumbotron to her right. The YouTube video of her and Rennen sparring was playing on a loop. Words like *kapow* and *splat* had been added in key parts, making the footage look like an old episode of Spiderman. She wished they'd quit playing that stupid video over and over. Every time she watched it, all she could see was the adventure dancing in Rennen's eyes as they squared off. That was the look that stole her heart—the challenge that made her want to rise up and meet him on every level.

Rennen was late. Maybe he wasn't coming. She swallowed her disappointment, trying to tell herself that it didn't matter. Things had been much simpler when they had their first sparring match. She'd been so upset because she'd fallen for the guy who was taking Ace's place on the Titans, never dreaming that was the least of her worries. After the fight with Rennen the day before, she'd sent Paul packing and was on the sofa, bawling, by the time Ace got to her apartment.

She gave Ace the same spiel she'd given Rennen, saying how Rennen was always waiting for everyone to disappoint him and how she couldn't live like that. She'd expected Ace to agree with her and was surprised when he came back with, "Give the guy a break. After all he's been through, it's a miracle he's doing as well as he is. It's obvious that Rennen loves you as much as you love him. Don't let the past taint your future. You're better than this anger. Quit being so dang stubborn." When she tried to argue, he wagged a finger, giving her a look that cut her to the quick. "You know I'm right. When Rennen calls or comes over to apologize—and he will—let him make it right ... for both your sakes."

Deep down, she knew Ace was right and was prepared to make up with Rennen. But Ariana hadn't heard a word from him. She kept replaying the accusation in his eyes, hearing his hateful words. Maybe the two of them had been doomed before they ever really got started. After all, Rennen had some hefty baggage to sift through. And she was at a loss as to how to help him.

She tightened her grip against the gauze and tape she'd wrapped around her hands. Her stomach felt queasy, partly due to the upcoming sparring match and partly due to her emotional state. She focused on breathing, hoping her training would take over. No hope of that!

Her blood pressure shot through the roof when Rennen came trotting across the field, the smile of a champion plastered over his handsome face. He really did look like a Titan from Greek Mythology with his curls gleaming like burnished gold in the afternoon sun, his body chiseled to perfection. Was this the same broken man who'd left her apartment the day before? What in the heck happened to bring about this dramatic change? She scowled, a burst of anger running through her. It wasn't right that he should be so composed when she was a wreck.

He climbed into the ring, pumping his fist to the crowd. The song

"We Are the Champions" by Queen boomed through nearby speakers as the audience went wild. Cartoon caricatures of Ariana and Rennen danced across the Jumbotron, boxing each other.

Rennen flashed a dazzling smile, his eyes roving over her in a leisurely way that unleashed a parade of butterflies in her stomach. "You look great."

She scowled. What was he up to? She moved to the opposite side of the ring from where Rennen was standing. He wouldn't be smiling when she knocked him on his butt.

The emcee, a local celebrity who had his own sports talk show, stepped into the ring holding a microphone. He was dressed in a black tuxedo with shiny, black shoes to match.

"Hello, everyone," he boomed. "I'm Marshall Sanders, your host for this event. Let's give it up for Rennen Bradley and Ariana Sanchez for so graciously agreeing to a rematch on the very field where the first one took place."

Applause thundered around the field, sounding like a stampede of eager elephants.

Marshall held up a hand to quiet the crowd. "The rules are simple, folks. The first one who gets pinned on the mat for three seconds loses." He motioned at Rennen and Ariana. "Come on now. Don't be shy."

They stepped up and bumped fists.

Marshall ducked through the ropes, stepping out of the ring. He looked over at the officials sitting behind a long table. "Do we have some sort of bell?"

A referee stepped into the ring as a loud buzzer sounded.

"There you go," Marshall boomed, a smile larger than The Grand Canyon splitting his face. "It's on."

Ariana crouched in fighting position, her blood pumping like a steam engine through her veins. A stupid grin washed over Rennen's face as he stepped up to her.

He raised his eyebrows. "This is gonna be fun."

His voice held the husky hint of promise, sending an unbidden tremble down her spine. She hated the effect he had on her. "You won't think it's so fun when I knock you on your butt," she muttered. She lunged at him, but he neatly sidestepped her attempt, sending her rushing into the ropes where she had to catch herself from falling. She spun around, glaring at him. Her anger was making her clumsy.

He only laughed.

She'd forgotten how fast Rennen was. *Sheesh*, he really was like a ghost—so smooth he almost glided. They circled around, eyeing each other.

"Come on," he taunted. "Make your move." His eyes danced. "And the more full-body contact the better."

"Pig," she muttered, remembering their previous conversation about this very thing. "We can't keep dancing around like this all day. One of us has to act."

He grinned. "Ladies first."

She let out a guttural growl as she rushed at him. She punched, her fist connecting with his jaw. He grunted in surprise. She followed the hit with a kick, but he deflected it.

"Good one," he said.

He jabbed at her, but she slapped his arm in a classic deflection move. They went a few more rounds before she realized Rennen wasn't really trying. This angered her more than anything.

"Come on," she yelled. "Don't hold back just because I'm a girl."

"Oh, I wouldn't dream of it," Rennen said pleasantly.

She went to sock him again, but he caught her arm and spun her around. He held her in a grip—so tight she felt like bands of steel were binding her. She tried to dig her heel into his foot but he moved it with a laugh. "Won't work this time. I've got your moves memorized. See ... full-body contact," he murmured, his warm breath tickling her ear. "Have you had enough?"

"Never," she said fiercely, collapsing to her knees. The move took Rennen by surprise as he fell forward, knocking them both to the mat. Ariana turned, facing him. They wrestled around on the mat, each trying to get the upper hand. Energy pulsed through Ariana like a live wire, making her feel alive and completely in the moment.

"You're pretty tough, for such a little thing," Rennen said admiringly, mischief sparking in his eyes.

"Oh, you haven't seen anything yet." Ariana kept slinging punches with Rennen dodging them. She tried to put him in an armbar, but his freaking arm was too strong.

"Have you given any thought to us?"

Ariana let out an incredulous laugh. "You're bringing this up now?" She had to draw back to keep from being put in a headlock.

"Sure, why not? I have your undivided attention."

She gritted her teeth. "If you wanted to talk about us, you should've had the decency to call or stop by." She couldn't keep the hurt from sounding in her voice.

"I would have, but I was a little busy ... making up with my mom."

The breath left her lungs. "W-what?" Hope sprang in her breast, and with it came a burst of energy. If Rennen had worked through that, then maybe they weren't doomed. She broke out of his grasp and jumped to her feet, whirling around to face him.

Rennen also got to his feet. But the second he did, Ariana side-swept his leg, sending him tumbling backwards. She jumped on top of him, pinning him down on the mat. She squeezed his arms with all she was worth, her knees pressing into each side of his waist to give her leverage.

The referee stood over them. "One ... two ... three," he shouted.

The crowd stood and cheered. Ariana felt the swell of victory then saw the hint of laughter in Rennen's eyes and realized with a start that he'd let her win—had probably let her win the first time too. She peered into his eyes. "You really made up with your mom?"

An unencumbered smile split his lips, sending a ray of sunshine shooting into her heart. "Yep, sure did. In fact, she's here." He motioned with his head to the left. Ariana looked over and saw Delphine and Thomas sitting two rows from the front. Heat burned up her neck as she thought about her predicament—on top of Rennen, pinning him down, in front of the all these people ... and Rennen's mom. If her own mother saw her right now, she'd be mortified. She moved to get off Rennen, but he slid his arms around her waist, pulling her back down. "What're you doing?" she grunted.

"What I should've done yesterday," he uttered. In a flash, he turned so that he was on top of her.

"You're such a pig," she muttered indignantly before his lips came down on hers. She fought against the kiss for an instant. "Not here," she tried to say, but the familiar flame licked through her as she returned his kiss with an urgency that surprised her. He pulled away, getting to his feet. Then he held out a hand, helping her to her feet.

His eyes lit with victory as a smile tipped his lips. "Now that's what I call a sparring match."

A smile curved her lips. "You talk big for a guy who just got whooped."

Rennen crouched into a fighting position, grinning. "Care to go for round two? Double or nothing?"

She made a face. "Are you serious?"

A reckless glint came into his eyes. "For real this time."

Adrenaline rushed through her veins. "All right. I'm game." She balled her fist and socked him, her hand making a loud pop as it connected with his jaw. He fell to his knees, then curled into a fetal position.

Alarm trickled down Ariana's spine. She'd not hit him that hard, had she?

She leaned over and touched his shoulder. "Are you okay?"

When he didn't move, she shoved him. "Rennen." Her throat went thick with fear. She about jumped out of her skin when he got up on one knee and reached for her hands. A picture flashed on the Jumbotron as piano music began playing. At first, Ariana didn't get it. Then everything became clear as tears brimmed in her eyes. The picture was a black and white photo of Rennen, holding up a large poster that read, *I'm sorry.*

His gaze held hers. "Just me and you ... no distractions ... only what really matters. I love you, and I want you in my life. Please give us another chance. I promise, I won't let you down."

"I love you too," she uttered, tears rolling down her cheeks. She let out a half-laugh. "I'm sorry I'm so stubborn."

He stood, arms encircling her waist. "And I'm sorry I've been too stupid to realize all the blessings I have in my life ... starting with you."

She stood on her tiptoes, lifting her face to his. A thunderous applause broke out across the stadium as their lips connected. Ariana slid her arms around Rennen's neck letting the feel of his lips overtake her, drowning out all else.

EPILOGUE

Six months later ...

Ariana wrinkled her nose as she looked across the table at Rennen and Ace. "You sure this is a good idea?"

Ace hooted, his voice taking on an exaggerated Mexican accent. "Yeah, wedo, you should listen to your woman. I don't think your delicate stomach can handle more than a couple of these tamales."

"We'll see about that, amigo," Rennen snorted. He patted his stomach, a cocky smile sliding over his lips. "I've got a gut of steel, and I'm about to prove it."

Ace chuckled. "That's what you said last week, when I roasted your butt in sprints."

Rennen pulled a face. "That was luck. Besides, my body's worn-out from the Titan's season." His eyes sparkled, a teasing grin tugging at his lips. "You know, winning the Championship Game was tough, man."

Ace scowled. "Yeah, you keep telling yourself that, wedo. Whatever helps you sleep at night." He looked at Ariana. "You sure you wanna marry this guy? His ego's the size of Texas."

A smile played on Ariana's lips as she looked down at the humongous rock on her finger. "Well, I guess I could hock this thing and make a small fortune."

Rennen clutched his chest. "Ouch. Now that hurt."

"Just teasing. I guess I have to keep him." Her eyes locked with Rennen's as a surge of electricity raced through her. Then came the wave of tenderness.

The past six months had been a whirlwind with the renovations at the gym and Rennen's winning season. But they had also been glorious. Ariana was so in love with Rennen she could hardly breathe. They were getting married in the spring. Her mother was overjoyed to be able to plan the wedding, but her ideas were so grand, they bordered on outlandish, reminding Ariana of the movie *My Big Fat Greek Wedding*. While it was a constant battle to make sure the wedding would be tasteful and elegant, Ariana was glad her family was so excited about the event. Everyone had welcomed Rennen into the family with open arms. And despite the fact that Rennen and Ace were always competing for the top-dog position, Ariana could tell they were close.

Delphine purchased a condo in Ft. Worth so she would have a place to stay during her frequent visits. Thomas accompanied her on her trips. Delphine and Thomas were so close that Ariana was starting to think Thomas was more than just her chauffeur. They'd not brought their relationship out in the open yet, but Ariana suspected that was coming in the near future. She chuckled inwardly. If Fabiana had anything to do with it, Delphine and Thomas would be married by the summer. She had taken one look at them and deemed them two, timid souls in need of a helping hand to bring them together as a couple.

Now that Rennen's season was over, he and Ariana were planning a trip to the Hamptons to visit Delphine. Rennen asked his mother who his father was, but she told him some things were better left in the past. Ariana knew Rennen well enough to know that he wouldn't be satisfied with that answer forever; but for now, he was willing to let it ride while he strengthened his relationship with Delphine. The change that had taken place in Rennen was remarkable. He seemed more complete and settled.

Silver put a hand on Ariana's arm. "You might as well sit back and relax." She pointed to the large platter of tamales in the center of the table. "Those two aren't going anywhere."

"I know, and Mom's in the kitchen making more tamales," Ariana said.

It was comical how fast Rennen and Ace's eyes bulged.

"Seriously?" Ace asked. "I thought Mom was watching Gracie and little Ace."

"Yeah, they're in the kitchen, but Dad's watching them while Mom's cooking," Ariana said straight-faced, but then couldn't hold back the laugh. "Just teasing," she quipped.

Rennen sighed in relief.

Silver pushed back her chair. "Speaking of the kids, I'd better check on them." She chuckled. "You know how much Gracie loves fried ice cream. She'll eat Fabiana out of house and home."

"I doubt that very seriously," Ariana said. "Mom has enough food in that kitchen to feed ten armies."

Silver just shook her head and smiled as she walked away.

It was fun to see Ace and Silver with two children, now that Silver'd had her baby. Fabiana was tickled pink to have another grandchild and kept hinting to Ariana and Rennen that they should start their family right after they were married, so she could have another grandchild.

Rennen rubbed his hands together. "Let the eating begin."

"You're going down, wedo," Ace said.

They looked at Ariana.

"Give us the signal to start," Ace prompted. "And remember, you're the moderator." He glanced at Rennen. "But don't be giving your man any preferential treatment."

"Oh, I wouldn't dream of it," Ariana said, her gaze locking with Rennen's.

Rennen's eyes danced with adventure. "She's telling the truth. She won't cut me an ounce of slack."

A bubble of sheer happiness broke in her chest, spreading warmth through her. "Someone has to keep you in line."

A smile tugged at Rennen's lips, his eyes caressing hers. "And you're the perfect one for the job."

"Absolutely."

A full smile broke over his lips. "I love you, babe."

She smiled back. Life was good! Oh, so good. "I love you too." She leaned forward, excitement trickling down her spine. "Ready, set ... go!"

READ THE HOMETOWN GROOM, the next book in Jennifer's Texas Titan Romances Series.

GET YOUR FREE BOOK

Hey there, thanks for taking the time to read *The Ghost Groom* from the Texas Titan Romance Series. If you enjoyed it, please take a minute to give me a review on Amazon. I really appreciate your feedback, as I depend largely on word of mouth to promote my books.

The Ghost Groom is a stand-alone novel, but you'll also enjoy reading the other books in Jennifer's Texas Titan Romance Series.

The Persistent Groom

The Ghost Groom

The Hometown Groom

The Jilted Billionaire Groom

Just a quick note—you may have noticed that my spelling of wedo (Ace's nickname for Rennen in the epilogue) was a bit unusual. Language is always tricky. The correct spelling is güero. However, I wanted to make sure everyone understood what Ace was saying, so I took liberties and used the phonetic spelling. I hope it didn't throw too many people off, especially those from Texas.

To receive updates when more of my books are coming out, sign up for my newsletter at http://jenniferyoungblood.com/

If you sign up for my newsletter, I'll give you one of my books, Beastly Charm: A contemporary retelling of beauty & the beast, for FREE. Plus, you'll get information on discounts and other freebies. For more information, visit:

http://bit.ly/freebookjenniferyoungblood

EXCERPT OF THE HOMETOWN GROOM
(TEXAS TITAN ROMANCES)

It wouldn't be easy to slip away from the barbecue undetected with the army of extra staff on the ranch. If her mama found out what was happening, she'd go berserk. Especially today, during the barbecue. Emerson scowled thinking of the dozens upon dozens of workers her mama had hired to put on the annual Stein Barbecue, an event that ranked right up there with the Lone Star Cattlemen's Ball.

No expense was spared. Mama had planned the details for months. An endless procession of catering vans streamed into the ranch over the past several days. They set up white tents with tables and seating, along with a giant barbecue station to prepare various cuts of beef from the ranch. Stein Ranch took pride in raising the finest Black Angus cattle in Texas. At the rate the chefs were cooking, there would be enough food to feed the entire population of Texas.

This year, the barbecue was especially significant because Emerson's older brother Graham would announce his bid for the Texas Senate. Meanwhile, Emerson was expected to look pretty and cast adoring glances at Finley Landers—the man her parents had selected for her to marry. She frowned at her reflection in the mirror. Anyone who thought arranged marriages were a thing of the past was sorely mistaken. The more prominent the family, the more stringent the requirements.

Emerson and Finley were childhood friends, even sweethearts for a time. But that faded to friendship years ago when Finley went to Yale and Emerson stayed home to attend Texas Christian University. Unfortunately, Finley was still smitten and wanted to marry her. "Too bad that's not gonna happen." She sighed heavily, applying a coat of cinnamon lipstick before dusting her cheekbones with bronzer. For the barbecue, she'd kept her makeup light, hair flat enough to keep her mama happy. Caroline Stein detested big hair, said it made girls look low class. Once Emerson arrived at the rodeo and dressed in her barrel racing clothes, she'd fluff up her hair and put on brighter lipstick and heavier makeup, more in keeping with her stage persona, Starr Andrews. Just because she wore a cowboy hat and raced full speed around barrels didn't mean she couldn't look good in the process. And contrary to her mama's opinion, Emerson happened to like bigger hair. Maybe not eighties style big, but big enough for her to feel feminine and pretty.

Caroline would die if she knew her daughter was barrel racing. Emerson hated deceiving her parents, but her mama was determined to mold her into a high-society debutante. Time and time again, Emerson told her parents that she had no intention of marrying Finley Landers. No way was she going to become a mini Caroline Stein, wasting her life away at social events, hobnobbing with the VIPs of the world. Emerson got her degree in business. She worked as an office manager in a veterinary clinic right now and planned to one day take over the family ranch, putting her education to good use. Of course, she'd have to find a way to convince her daddy of that. In his mind, Emerson would always be his little girl.

Emerson ran a brush through her long red hair, pushing aside the intrusive thoughts. She needed to focus on tonight's race, an open jackpot, meaning it was open to all contestants regardless of race or gender. Those were Emerson's favorite. She could simply compete without as much red tape. For her, the money didn't matter. It was the thrill of the ride that counted. Those few seconds in the arena, she felt alive and completely in control of her life ... as opposed to all the other times when she was her mama's puppet.

A knock at the door caused her to jump. "Emerson," her mama ordered, "open the door. We need to talk."

Crap! "I'm coming," she yelled, grabbing the duffel bag from the center of the bed and shoving it in her closet. She took in a breath and straightened her shoulders, walking slowly to the door.

Her mama stepped in, eagle eyes sweeping the room with suspicion. "Why did you lock the door?"

"I didn't realize I had," Emerson said lightly. She hated the way Mama looked her up and down, like she was trying to find something wrong.

"I thought you were wearing the green sundress. It goes better with your eyes."

Emerson glanced down at the dress in question. "I decided to wear the blue one instead." *Geez.* Couldn't the woman give her an inch of space to be her own person? She was twenty-five years old, for goodness' sake. Things had been so much simpler when she had her own place.

She jutted out her chin, glaring at her mama who was dressed impeccably in a black dress and matching heels, her copper hair wound in a chic French twist. It had sheen to it, making Emerson wonder which hair product her mama had used to get that effect. Ironic that Emerson looked so much like her mama, yet their personalities were opposite. Five feet six inches tall, Caroline Stein was as lean as she'd been in her twenties. Like Emerson, she had freckles dusted over her nose, lively green eyes, and a sparkling white smile—the girl next door with a touch of glamour.

Caroline sat down on the bed and patted the space next to her. Reluctantly, Emerson sat down. "I don't have to tell you how important today is," she began, "with Graham's announcement."

Emerson groaned inwardly. *Here we go again.* "I know that, Mama." Graham was the perfect son, happy to mold himself into the narrow expectations of their mama. He'd gone to Harvard, found himself a Jaqueline Kennedy wife, blue-bred with an Ivy League degree of her own. Jenna was well-dressed with a conservative hair-style. She always knew the proper thing to say in any given situation, was fiercely devoted to Graham and his career, making sure they associated with only the right people. And, she'd given him two sons.

Not that it was a competition. Too bad Emerson couldn't convince her mama of that. Her favorite sentence was, "If only you were more like Graham."

"I need for you to be on your best behavior."

She swallowed the incredulous laugh in her throat. "Oh, that's too bad. I was thinking about taking my clothes off and streaking across the ranch right after the announcement."

"No need to get smart," Caroline snapped.

Emerson rolled her eyes, feeling a smidgen of remorse for the catty remark. "Don't worry, Mama. I won't embarrass you."

When Caroline gave her a doubtful look, the words spilled out. "I'll wear an insipid smile and pretend to be impressed by all of your dull friends."

A flash of anger moved over Caroline's face, followed by a wounded look. "Why must you always be so coarse? I came in here to have a simple conversation, not to fight."

Therein was the problem. They were never starting at square one. Every conversation carried the remains of previous jabs. Maybe Emerson was being too hard on her mama. After all, she did have some good qualities. Hmm ... what were those qualities? Well, she was beautiful ... took great care of herself. Emerson hoped she looked half that good when she got to be her mama's age. And she loved Emerson's dad Ethan. Of course, it didn't hurt that he was worth millions. Caroline was fiercely protective of her family, which would be good if the flip side of that wasn't her trying to control every little thing in Emerson's life. She let out a long sigh. "I'm sorry," she said, mostly to get the conversation over with. "I promise I'll be on my best behavior." *For the thirty or so minutes I'm there*, she added mentally. After that she was skipping out to the rodeo.

Caroline looked her in the eye. "I want you to be nicer to Finley. Show him some interest."

This time, Emerson couldn't hold back the chortle in her throat. It came out sounding scratchy and hollow. "What?" Okay, her mama was going too far.

"Finley's handsome, charming, well-educated, and crazy about you. Why can't you show him some affection? Throw him a bone, for heaven's sake!"

Emerson's eyes bugged as she clutched her throat, surprised there was no noose around it because it certainly felt that way. "Because I don't love him."

"Love will come ... eventually. But you have to give it a chance."

Disgust sat like rotten potatoes in Emerson's stomach. "This isn't about love. It's about the merger." In two months, Stein Cattle Ranch was joining forces with Landers Technology. The merger would not only unite one of the largest cattle ranches in Texas with a cutting-edge software and analytics company that could revolutionize the agriculture industry, but it would join two powerful families, creating an unstoppable economic force. Finley's family, the Landers, were billionaires who had a long history in oil refining. The past decade, their interests had morphed into natural oil, wind energy, and software development. Kenton Landers was itching to put his new software into practice, first with the Stein Ranch and then with ranches and farms all over the country.

"It's about your future," Caroline said smoothly.

Emerson's eyebrows shot up. "Don't you mean your future?" She could tell from the way Caroline started blinking that she'd hit the nail on the head. "Tell me, Mama, what'll happen to the merger if I don't get engaged to Finley?"

Caroline touched her hair, letting out a long sigh. "Must you be so insolent all the time?"

Insolent? Mama always used fancy words when she got upset. "I'm not a piece of livestock, to be sold off to the highest bidder. I've told you and Daddy, when I marry, it'll be for love." She clenched her jaw. "The sooner y'all get that through your heads, the better."

Fire sparked in Caroline's eyes. "You're being handed the opportunity of a lifetime, and you're throwing it away." She lifted her chin, a hard edge coming into her voice. "I'll not allow you to ruin everything."

No matter how many times Emerson shouted from the rooftop that she wasn't marrying Finley Landers, it didn't seem to sink into her mama's head. Emerson balled her fists, wanting to punch something. "I'm an adult, Mama. Not a kid. You don't control me."

Caroline's eyes burned into hers. "You be nice to Finley. Do you hear me?" she hissed.

"Of course, I'll be nice to him. I always am. But I won't pretend to feel something I don't. You know what? I knew it was a mistake to move back home. I should've stayed in my apartment." She had a good job, more than enough money to pay her own way ten times over.

"Don't be ridiculous. Your place is here with us. You know how much it means to your daddy to have you here, especially with his health being so tenuous."

Yes, she did. Which is the primary reason Emerson agreed to move back home. Her daddy had been diagnosed with Type 2 Diabetes. It had been serious, his sugar through the roof. Thankfully, his medicine was getting it under control. Now that her daddy was better, Emerson dropped hints about wanting to get another place of her own. Every time she brought it up, her parents went into a flurry, listing all the reasons she should stay. Eventually, Emerson would have to bite the bullet and move out. It was brutal dealing with her mama on a daily basis.

They sat glaring at one another. Finally, Caroline stood. "I've some last-minute items I need to take care of before the barbecue starts." She gave Emerson a withering look. "Do us both a favor. Wear the green dress. The one you have on makes you look like you have a flat tire around your waist." With that, she tromped out and slammed the door behind her.

Tears gathered in Emerson's eyes. Quickly, she blinked them away. The dress she had on was perfectly fine. The flat tire comment was Mama's way of controlling her. She stood and looked at her reflection in the mirror. To her horror, she realized that the dress did make her look a little thick around the middle. She sucked in her stomach assessing herself. "Dang you, Mama," she muttered, peeling off the dress and tossing it into the corner as she went to her closet to get the green one.

Continue reading Here.

BOOKS BY JENNIFER YOUNGBLOOD

Check out Jennifer's Amazon Page:
http://bit.ly/jenniferyoungblood

Georgia Patriots Romance
The Hot Headed Patriot
The Twelfth Hour Patriot

O'Brien Family Romance
The Impossible Groom (Chas O'Brien)
The Twelfth Hour Patriot (McKenna O'Brien)
Rewriting Christmas (A Novella)
Yours By Christmas (Park City Firefighter Romance)
Her Crazy Rich Fake Fiancé

Navy SEAL Romance
The Resolved Warrior
The Reckless Warrior
The Diehard Warrior

The Jane Austen Pact

Seeking Mr. Perfect

Texas Titan Romances

The Hometown Groom

The Persistent Groom

The Ghost Groom

The Jilted Billionaire Groom

The Impossible Groom

The Perfect Catch (Last Play Series)

Hawaii Billionaire Series

Love Him or Lose Him

Love on the Rocks

Love on the Rebound

Love at the Ocean Breeze

Love Changes Everything

Loving the Movie Star

Love Under Fire (A Companion book to the Hawaii Billionaire Series)

Kisses and Commitment Series

How to See With Your Heart

Angel Matchmaker Series

Kisses Over Candlelight

The Cowboy and the Billionaire's Daughter

Romantic Thrillers

False Identity

False Trust

Promise Me Love

Burned

Contemporary Romance

Beastly Charm

Fairytale Retellings (The Grimm Laws Series)
    Banish My Heart **(This book is FREE)**
    The Magic in Me
    Under Your Spell
    A Love So True

Southern Romance
    Livin' in High Cotton
    Recipe for Love

The Second Chance Series
    Forgive Me (Book 1)
    Love Me (Book 2)

Short Stories
    The Southern Fried Fix

ABOUT JENNIFER YOUNGBLOOD

Jennifer loves reading and writing clean romance. She believes that happily ever after is not just for stories. Jennifer enjoys interior design, rollerblading, clogging, jogging, and chocolate. In Jennifer's opinion there are few ills that can't be solved with a warm brownie and scoop of vanilla-bean ice cream.

Jennifer grew up in rural Alabama and loved living in a town where "everybody knows everybody." Her love for writing began as a young teenager when she wrote stories for her high school English teacher to critique.

Jennifer has BA in English and Social Sciences from Brigham Young University where she served as Miss BYU Hawaii in 1989. Before becoming an author, she worked as the owner and editor of a monthly newspaper named *The Senior Times*.

She now lives in the Rocky Mountains with her family and spends her time writing and doing all of the wonderful things that make up the life of a busy wife and mother.

For more information:
www.jenniferyoungblood.com
authorjenniferyoungblood@gmail.com

f facebook.com/authorjenniferyoungblood
🐦 twitter.com/authorjennı
📷 instagram.com/authorjenniferyoungblood

Made in the USA
San Bernardino, CA
20 March 2020

66055916R00122